ISBN: 978-1-4092-3096-0

Coherent Madness: Effective Defense Against Covert Warfare

"Believe nothing, no matter where you read it, or who said it, no matter if I have said it, unless it agrees with your own reason and your own common sense."

Buddha (563BC-483BC).

Contents at a Glance

Introduction	....	1
Chapter 1:	Prologue...	3
Chapter 2:	Who are these people?...................................	13
Chapter 3:	What are The Attack Methods?.....................	33
Chapter 4:	Why do People Become Targets of Covert Warfare?..	39
Chapter 5:	Dispelling Doubt..	59
Chapter 6:	Keeping Accounts...	79
Chapter 7:	Securing Your Home......................................	83
Chapter 8:	Blocking Directed Energy Weapons Attacks............	99
Chapter 9:	Securing External Property............................	115
Chapter 10:	Safety While Out and About.........................	119
Chapter 11:	Mental and Physical Health...........................	131
Chapter 12:	Conclusion...	145
Bibliography	....	149
Glossary	....	155

Table of Contents

Introduction	....	**1**
Chapter 1:	**Prologue.**...	**3**
Chapter 2:	**Who Are These People?.**.........................	**13**
	Historical Parallels...	13
	Personality Profile of the Average Gang Member..............	14
	Organization: Hierarchy and Connections......................	22
	Institutionalization of Covert Warfare..........................	27
Chapter 3:	**What are The Attack Methods?**................	**33**
	Psychological Harassment......................................	33
	Direct Physical Violence..	36
Chapter 4:	**Why People Become Targets of Covert Warfare.**.......	**39**
	Pre-emptive Strategy: Potential Threat Elimination..........	39
	Mentacide: Deliberate Destruction of the Mind................	42
	Relational and Other Problems................................	56
	Xenophobic and Racial...	58
	Political and Economic...	58
Chapter 5:	**Dispelling Doubt.**....................................	**59**
	Clearing the Fog Of Doubt.....................................	62
	Weighing Security System Vulnerabilities.....................	67
	Personalized Security Systems.................................	71
	Last Resort: the Mobile Home.................................	75
Chapter 6:	**Keeping Accounts.**...................................	**79**
	Poison Deposit Zones...	79
	Other Personal Accounts.......................................	80
Chapter 7:	**Securing Your Home.**...............................	**83**
	Contaminants in Solids and Liquids...........................	85
	Airborne Attacks..	93
Chapter 8:	**Blocking Directed Energy Weapon Attacks.**...........	**99**
	History...	103
	How DEW work..	105
	Obstruction..	106
Chapter 9:	**Securing External Property.**......................	**115**
Chapter 10:	**Safety While Out and About.**.....................	**119**
	Staying Alert When You Mingle...............................	119
	Securing Your Shopping..	126
	Going on the Run...	127
Chapter 11:	**Mental and Physical Health.**......................	**131**

	Health Check and Medication..................................	131
	Meditation Based Healing.......................................	133
	Physical Exercise...	134
	Healthy Mental Attitude...	137
Chapter 12:	**Conclusion.**.......................................	**145**
Bibliography	....	**149**
Glossary	....	**155**

Introduction

I will take it for granted you already know, or have heard of people who died of what were natural causes, deaths that nonetheless raised suspicion among some people due to one anomaly or another. I will assume you know of cases where men and women, mostly activists, who were in their prime at the time, suddenly succumbed to an unlikely terminal affliction, or some other condition, be this from a sudden stroke, rapid growth of a terminal cancer, etc. Others may have taken their lives, and still some met their end through sudden, sometimes accidental, often gratuitous violence. In most social circles, especially among some races, the number of incidences of death under suspicious circumstances is indeed significant, and occurrences of such deaths repetitive enough for there to be a discernible pattern, for there to be justifiable talk of not only foul play, but a hidden agenda.

As a man who has over a prolonged period been a target of covert warfare by groups of people unknown to me, for reasons I have only recently grasped, I intend to prove that I, and an ever increasing number of people bringing forth similar accounts, are in fact survivors of a method of elimination that claimed some of the deaths considered before, a method of attack carefully designed to appear like the victim was not murdered, but died of natural causes, or unfortunate accident.

These accounts, especially the fact they have similar points of convergence, point to peculiar methods that have been adopted by law enforcement, governments, and corporations globally to eliminate those who pose a threat to them. Additionally, they imply knowledge gained through scientific research, spying and elimination methods and technologies mostly developed for the purpose of war, are now being used not to keep real enemies at bay, or to fight justified wars against threats to human freedom, but to eliminate innocent civilians, especially those who think for themselves, those who ask questions.

I will then proceed to share knowledge I have gained through my ordeal, in what has been a trying and lengthy game of cat and mouse between my stalkers and me, which hopefully teaches effective methods of coping, if not defeating covert warfare.

Keep an open mind as you go along so that you avoid jumping to conclusions, because what I will write down in this book will readily resemble a lot of states and conditions that can easily stand in as viable explanations. This is unfortunately a part of the strategy of such attacks; this is what has made this method of elimination so successful to date. People who have never been exposed to certain realities seldom phantom the possibility, making them prone to rely on what they know to explain what they are hearing or seeing. I remind you that you do not have to wait until you, a close or loved one, gets into a situation from which you cannot escape before you take actions that protect you from the full force of such attacks. You do not have to become a victim of, for example, the real habit of housing agencies in many developed countries to relocate a blacklisted individual to neighborhoods inhabited exclusively by people employed by such criminals, turning your daily life into a nightmare, or prison. You do not have to wait until you or a loved one is attacked by a criminal in the employ of these people, or gets a sudden and inexplicable physical condition before you take this seriously.

Browse through this book and take mental notes as these will prove useful in situations you may be confronted with in real life. Learn of the various methods employed in this elimination process, learn of the extent even innocuous social institutions have been infiltrated, as this will be vital in helping you identify situations where you could fall into a trap. You should especially know who qualifies for covert government harassment or elimination so you know where you, and the various personalities of those you know or will bring forth, stand.

If you do not see yourself bending to the kind of pressure those who want to keep you in the dark and in bondage will bring to bear on you to maintain or achieve this state, because you are convinced you are doing the right thing; or see the possibility someone you know will inevitably end up a victim, then you need to learn how to build a strong defense against what is as such an imminent threat. Have this information handy, to share or use for self should it become necessary. These measures against covert attack do not need actual proof of the activity to be set up, just as you would never wait to be robbed before you install security equipment. Knowing of the possibility should be a good enough incentive.

Chapter 1

Prologue

Overt surveillance that I first experienced as "ready recognition" whenever I was out and about in Western Europe, especially in areas I had never visited before, is the first thing that told me I was under unprecedented surveillance in this part of the world. I had never before known the kind of attention I suddenly aroused whenever I appeared in public places in any other country. I know for a fact that when I was in Russia, in Poland, in Czechoslovakia, Tunisia, Bulgaria, or back home in Africa, I was not as readily recognized in public as when I came to Germany, Holland, Italy, France and England.

I am not referring to the extra attention physical deformity, disease or such, attracts, that I would easily have identified because, by nature, a lot of people are unguarded enough to eventually let the one being watched know; but recognition on account of familiarity, especially the kind that occurs in a new locality where you do not know anybody yet, where you have not done anything yet, and have not had the time to show signs you are about to do anything.

There were indeed times when some people pointed out physical abnormalities or affliction as the cause of the overt surveillance, a premise that became at once questionable in light of various related issues. In fact, the manner they would intimate such a state itself made the attempt obvious as a distraction, if not an excuse, rather than the cause.

Occurring simultaneously with these events was, for example, the occasional steep rise in the level of anger expressed, and threats made by strangers whenever I wrote an article that got published, the very same types who would divulge personal information whenever they got the chance, that revealed there was more to the overt surveillance than physical state alone. For me at the time, these moments of unguarded reaction, when those persecuting me would bare their fangs in reaction to what I had done, provided the crucial evidence of what the actual problem was. They provided proof this whole exercise was nothing but an attempt to mould my very personality.

The phenomenon didn't start out in the pronounced manner described before as soon as I arrived in the west, but gradually built up to levels where it became abnormal, to the point when a single walk through an unknown area would elicit public responses that revealed immediate recognition, that in rare instances would be confirmed by the odd indirect reference to what was really going on; for example when personal information would be thrown at me in encounters with total strangers.

The recognition I am referring to cannot be confused with normal harassing/elimination activities usually associated with gangs who wage covert warfare on civilians. On the surface, stalking activity tends to resemble plain clothed police or secret service surveillance, with the exception the person being watched is not only made aware he/she is under surveillance, but is often harassed and intimidated, and at times attacked physically.

Surveillance by citizen harassment groups is limited by the fact normal, everyday people highly outnumber members of such gangs, making their activities small scale, whereas what I was experiencing in the west appeared to be coming from the entire population itself.

I knew for a fact that this recognition was absent in African communities throughout mainland Europe where I could mingle and not feel over watched, and, revealingly enough, was conspicuously absent among tourists coming from other European countries, including countries in Western Europe itself. For example, tourists from Italy in Germany would not recognize me in the same manner Germans did in areas I had never been to before within their country, and conversely, German tourists in Italy would be oblivious of my existence, while the Italians would be overly aware of my presence.

Logic dictates that if there was something visibly wrong with me, then tourists would also have noticed, no matter how overwhelmed they were by the novelty of their experience.

Because the overt surveillance followed me throughout Western Europe, the only logical explanation for the oblivious nature of tourists to my existence is that they became detached from the core of such surveillance in a different country. They became but a group of individuals who were not getting the kind of feedback from the new environment that would enable them to act and react in a certain way.

As mentioned already, this recognition was absent in countries outside the western sphere where I spent significant lengths of time, to the extent I can speak fluently in many languages, countries to which I intermittently returned to visit friends. Poland, for example, is a country inhabited almost exclusively by white people. Here, I could walk the streets for days on end feeling like a complete stranger to all who are strangers to me except the occasional person who would give me the kind of attention that pointed to as much recognition, as a need to let me know I was an undesirable on account of personality or race. Some of these occurrences are actually expected when you are a foreigner of a certain race in most societies around the globe, especially Europe where racism and surveillance are never far to find.

Soon, however, I would discover that though there were incredibly large segments of western society that knew more than would be considered normal in any other world society, the majority of them reacted more on cue from others rather than that they were in on some conspiracy. This means there was a group of people stalking me, whose activities would not be lost on the populace at large, who would in reaction watch the watched, some believing there was something the victim had done, a law they had broken, that had prompted overt surveillance from what they considered was the country's secret service. The phenomenon I had observed was in fact the combined effect of overt stalker activity and the reaction to it by the greater population.
Logically, I localized the phenomenon. At first I figured it was a reaction of figures in authority in that particular country to my presence there. I was naïve enough to think relocation would solve the problem, and found it hard to explain why the surveillance followed me wherever I went in western Europe, however low a profile I maintained, no matter how much I foolishly tried to obey some of the commands thrown at me by encounters with strangers on the streets; stopped writing, stopped engaging in activities I felt offended the sensibilities of locals, etc. I could also not understand why it did not follow me when I ventured outside of the western sphere, to other communities around the world.

Along the way however, the reality of my situation began to dawn on me. I soon developed a theory explaining who I believed was behind the stalking, the purpose, how the whole thing worked; why some people are selected while others are not, even when personalities are outwardly similar. Learning by personal exposure that it involved covert attacks aimed at maiming or eventual elimination, without leaving clues foul play was involved, dispelled any belief I had before that the harassment was meant to drive the target out of the town or country. I realized the combined effects of the attacks prevented the target from having either the mental, physical, even monetary means of escape, which could only be part of the plan.

I was astounded to discover how similar the theory I developed was to what has now become common knowledge of the machinations of citizen harassment and elimination, also called covert warfare, with the major difference being that I had concluded the source was a neo-colonial structure created to control Africans in general, therefore what I went through only applied to Africans living in the west and in countries that were former colonies. I learnt from victim testimonies that it applies to members of all ethnic groups.

It would be easy to conclude from this that I was mistaken, that there is no actual preference for race at all in all countries where such attacks occur, that no special structures have been set up for the control of minority groups where they exist.

This may indeed be true for most countries, but a lot of evidence points to the existence of a separate structure in especially western countries that have interests tied into minority populations, and other interests in those who live in areas where a lot of resources are derived, designed specifically for the detection and elimination of threats to the continuation of these advantages, and a lot of evidence points as well to the reality this structure is international and motivated by racialist beliefs.

A lot of evidence suggests this structure has all along operated not on the classic doctrine of the pre-emptive strategy, but the modern version made popular by the Bush administration where it is not limited to perceived threats, but to possibilities of their development. Threats need no longer be perceived before they are reacted to, but the potential for their development to levels where they can become perceivable threats needs to be checked.

Once initiated, this approach to problem solving knows no end. For example, a Malcolm X is considered a problematic character in this system. Preventing another Malcolm X from being created entails a combination of incapacitating attacks on all who show signs of becoming replica figures at points in their lives where they are not yet distinguished as such, after which it will be too late because another martyr would already have been created. Achieving this degree of early detection requires an increase in the levels of illegal activities that afford the capacity to affect the state on select individuals.

This would however be an ongoing process since the birth of such personalities is continuous. Unless the social conditions they react to change for the better, such characters will end up doing the very same that others before them did. Changing these very social conditions that they react to is a very good way of solving this problem, but the wrongs already committed against some groups, and the fact the maintenance of the present state is tied to tribal survival itself makes such an eventuality hard to imagine, if not impossible. In order not to make the task of suppressing such individuals overwhelming, other measures need to be implemented, especially those that either prevent their birth in the first place, or render them useless for the purpose from as early as birth.

General birth control would only be effective to a degree since the lessened population would still require to be controlled, not to mention genes are not only inherited, but sometimes recessive. There is the possibility the very same genes responsible for the creation of the characters being eliminated are lying dormant within the greater race to which they belong. This undetected potential could slip through the measures, finding expression in new births and developing into the feared personality when least expected. The entire race has therefore also got to be controlled in manners that weaken their seed, for example.

And so on.

One way the racist core at the center of the structure becomes evident is the vast majority of whites in western countries who fall victim to covert warfare are individuals who are lax with, or do not see race, who mingle freely, and are overly helpful to members of ethnic minorities. The overabundance of testimony by targeted individuals (TI) to this effect reveals the ranks of these citizen elimination gangs are infested with racists. To draw this conclusion requires knowledge that these gangs of men and women who attack and eliminate innocent people are answerable to higher, established authority. Their very existence and the impunity with which they operate depend on complicity from these higher levels.

The generally held belief extremist organizations like the Ku Klux Klan (KKK) refined this form of covert warfare by practice on American Africans, methods that were later adopted by stalking groups, is fallacious, as this would only be the case in a society where the need for research, the means to conduct such research, and the technology required is developed and exclusive to extremist segments of society, which is not the case. It can safely be argued the KKK, like the gangs of stalkers, learnt the methodology from higher levels of society, rather than that the citizen stalking groups learnt it from the KKK. Because these stalkers are merely carrying out orders from powerful segments of society, they become mere representatives of these, and the trend for them to be racist in their attacks must have a root in higher authority.

When I lived in mainland Europe, Africans would rarely be involved in these attack campaigns. As already mentioned, I would be left alone when I was in a predominantly African neighborhood, seen in the fact I never noticed the same level of recognition among locals as that in whites areas. This points to the reality the surveillance was not openly displayed in front of Africans, a fact with the potential to prompt the conclusion the whole thing was designed against African people. The reasoning here would be that the only reason those who followed me would keep a low profile in African communities is because Africans, unlike whites, would immediately recognize the activity as the attack against them that it was.

Only when I had lived for lengthy periods in a predominantly African neighborhood, and only due to the fact I made it hard for those following me to keep up, so that they were forced into ever more activities with the potential to reveal their intentions; and especially since such activities usually coincided with a visibly large influx of white residents to the particular area, did it become increasingly obvious to my new neighbors that I was under round the clock surveillance.

Once, after moving into a crime ridden, predominantly African neighborhood in Holland, I came upon a group of homeless people who had squatted some property near where I lived, who suddenly found themselves evicted a short while after my arrival. One day, as I was passing the group, I heard them debating the possibility I was to blame for their eviction. I had not gone a step past the group when the conclusion was voluminously and unanimously reached, with a touch of indignation, that I was indeed the reason the authorities had decided to take back that particular property for its strategic location. The group made sure I heard their point of view, also alerting me of my unwanted nature.

The fact they viewed me as the source of their problem has the potential to be exploited as a recruiting tool by members of stalking gangs. Recruits are usually those who are gullible enough, whose level of understanding is low enough for their universe to be focused on one location, so that they are convinced their problems are caused by the particular individual, and will only be solved once that person leaves the neighborhood.

What is sad about the skulduggery of the people who control these gangs is, along the way, the problems of these new recruits will indeed become connected to the TI. Whatever he/she will try to do to help self will succeed or fail according to how much their handler needs their services regarding the same individual, which usually means accruing complicity and having little choice but to accept moving on to a next case when asked.

It's only when I came to the United Kingdom that I met a significant number of Africans who would readily recognize me even in places where I had not ventured before, and would refer to issues that speak too specifically to those in my personal life in the same manner white stalkers in white communities did. Only in the UK did I for the first time come face to face with recognition in African communities that was close to that experienced in the majority white population in other European countries.

I have thus far failed to find an ideological motivation powerful enough to move Africans to such acts as it does a significant number of whites, especially the racists and extremists. I do know that many are in the business for money. Blackmail is also involved, especially on issues where a lot of Africans are known to be vulnerable, such as immigration status or fear of detention or deportation. There could also be esteem issues involved, such as the lure of the 007 myth. Otherwise they, like their white counterparts, and others who are used for the purpose worldwide, are severely misinformed about their targets.

The techniques employed in covert warfare on civilians are so subtle, surreptitious and alien to the imagination of the average citizen that, unless concrete evidence can be brought forth as proof; for example a voice recording or hidden camera footage that catches the perpetrators in the act, accounts by targets are more likely than not to be considered products of minds that have lost their grip on reality, if not that the target is blamed for attracting extra attention. Without hard evidence, it boils down to taking the victims word for it, but then depending upon the damage done to the TI's mind, the difference between latent or induced paranoia may become blurred, the capacity to be coherent may have been lost, the mental stamina required for effective communication may have been sapped, in which case attempts to communicate the experience may tend to work against the TI.

We are all only as good as the state of our mind. Our level of understanding, even uptake, derives from this. A mind that is gradually malnourished or worn down will result in the individual losing their power of comprehension without even being cognizant of this regression, unless they can test their cognitive skills using certain tools. Convictions once held may linger, but will eventually fade as the capacity to reason one's way to the conclusion that led to them disappears. This also means that issues that require the same level of intellectual skills to comprehend become more and more beyond reach. As a consequence, victims may unknowingly start to sound insane but believe they are making sense. They may start to sound as though they are making reality up as they go along, fantasizing. Because they are not aware of this mental degeneration, they may force the issue, harming their own cause as such.

The perpetrators of covert violence know this perfectly well, and are never at any point in the process passive players who await an outcome, especially not when victims attempt to communicate attack experiences to the general public. They remain active in every facet of this process, doing all they can to diminish the credibility of the victim.

These activities are not limited to attacks that take away from the verity of the targeted individual's accounts, such as the destruction of mental equilibrium accompanied by sabotage activities that accomplish the same, but how people in such situations are perceived in general. All it takes are a few individuals to pose as victims and relate evidently false experiences that are deliberately exaggerated and extended to include, for example, demons or aliens, to create in the public's mind the wrong impression about the general mental state of people who bring forth reports of this nature, putting them off believing the whole covert warfare phenomenon in the first place. The general public ends up writing the whole thing off as the deranged ranting of disturbed minds.

There are also unfortunately a lot of people in society who know such attacks are not fiction, and others who reach this conclusion by deduction, but then unfortunately conclude individuals targeted in this manner deserve the punishment because they are guilty of behavior or crimes that go against the good of society, behavior or crimes impossible to charge, change or punish through existing legal channels. Such people then believe what amounts to an extra- judicial system is necessary.

Due to the many awareness campaigns that have been launched to date, this state of affairs is fortunately, gradually giving way to more public awareness and acceptance. People are realizing such attacks are a reality, and that they are not always done for the good of the whole. The public is realizing that individuals singled out for covert attacks are usually not the problem.

It is slowly becoming accepted that this problem has been growing, the occurrence becoming more widespread and entrenched, to the extent we can speak of the existence in most countries today of stalking groups whose members actually make a lifestyle of attack activities on innocent civilians, which mostly consist of covert incapacitation, maiming, neutralization or elimination of selected individuals. These stalking gangs step in as judge, jury, and executioner of people who do not mean society at large any harm, but who, for one reason or another, are a threat to a group or groups in positions of responsibility, with the financial means and connections to make such campaigns possible.

The general trend, as some have observed, is to muzzle not the out of control segments of society; the dangerous criminals who cannot be brought to justice by existing means, but people who are asking questions, conducting bona fide research to find answers, or standing up for other people's or their human rights. The targets are as such positive minded, conscientious, and mostly sympathetic members of society.

It goes without saying that the more people know this is happening in society, the better it will turn out for everybody. The more people learn how to defend themselves against covert warfare, the less the chance the practice will continue. These criminal stalking gangs will be forced to think twice before launching covert attacks on citizens, meaning we will no longer be picked at will. Humankind will as such be rid of a thorn in its side causing so much discomfort in our time, preventing the resolution of pressing issues created and kept alive by the same parties who depend upon the practice of covert warfare to maintain barbarism, especially by the constant elimination of those who can make a difference.

This may get us closer to a time when a system infested with men and women who are worse criminals than those normally thrown behind bars; psychopaths of all kinds, shapes and sizes, the latter of whom would honestly be surprised what amateurs they are when exposed to the kind and scope of horror the former are capable of, that they unleash on a daily basis on unsuspecting multitudes, is expelled; if not that a negative institutional trend becomes the exception rather than the rule on a worldwide scale.

Chapter 2

Who Are These People?

In This Chapter
- Historical Parallels
- Personality Profile of the Average Gang Member
- Organization: Hierarchy and Connections
- Institutionalization of Covert Warfare

The name given to the phenomena of citizen stalking and harassment tends to change with time, circumstance, and methods. The common name used today is Gang-Stalking, or Predatory Gang-Stalking. Gaslighting, a term derived from the 1944 Hollywood movie "Gaslight" where like methods are employed to undermine an individual psychologically, is another. It is currently called "Hanging" in England.

R.B. Ross defines Predatory Gang-Stalking as *"a criminal phenomenon referring to a group of loosely affiliated people who, in an organized and systematic manner, relentlessly invade an individual's life on a continuous basis, to an extreme degree, as part of their lifestyle. While each individual Gang-Stalker does his or her small part, what defines Predatory Gang-Stalking is the collective intent to do harm"*.

Historical Parallels

Predatory Gangstalking is known to have been a common practice in the Christian church from where the alternate term "Cause-Stalking" is derived. Here, the harassment was intended to force sinners to repent, or drive undesirables out. The version that existed in the Germany of the 1930's was called "Jew baiting". Anti Jewish sentiments already run high in Germany before the "final solution". Prior to this, the police could not arrest a Jew for any reason whatsoever. Locals would however "bait" Jews into violent outbursts by subjecting them to systematic, sustained harassment. When the Jew reacted, he/she was accused of the crime, promptly arrested then sent to a concentration camp.

Similar methods of attack have been identified with extremist organizations. One example is the KKK in America that is known to have used covert warfare against American Africans. Some say they started and refined the practice, dating its inception back to the early 90's. Evidence exists that suggests the methods were in use way before this time. The American FBI's COINTELPRO program, set up to keep perceived threats in society in line, more especially communists and American Africans, targeting those who were considered ringleaders, even if potentially so, utilized the same methods to isolate, break, then eliminate not only perceived threats, but the remotest of potential for their creation. This program was so deep reaching it would take into account heredity, so that the direct descendants of those who had reacted to the system in certain ways were prone to be harassed, prevented from succeeding in life, or incapacitated in other ways, even when these individuals were not in the know of what their ancestors had done; only because such a link was seen to make them potential risks.

The practice is also known to have existed in the feudalistic era where it was known as "blacklisting". Here, rich families persecuted or prosecuted the poor or eliminated threats to their standing in society through similar methods of attack. Some argue that the very rich families of old are behind the present, rapid expansion of covert warfare. The present growth of the practice is then explained as being in part a continuation of an old activity, that's expanding and becoming highly visible in the present due to the mistrust and fear held by these families of the freedoms the populace at large currently enjoys, bolstered in large part by the advent of technology that makes inter-cultural and international communication and sharing of ideas possible. Their privileged position is under threat, so that they feel forced to use the back end of the system, accessible to them by virtue of their positioning, to launch covert campaigns against activities they perceive as threatening.

Personality Profile of the Average Gang Member

Unlike is the general tendency of stalking activities, perpetrators of Predatory Gangstalking crimes are not predominantly male, and the vast majority of their victims are not women, but men. In multiracial societies, they belong to no particular racial group, nor are they drawn from a particular social class, though evidence of the phenomenon in America, for example, suggests the majority of the victims are American African males.

A lot of targets report never ending disturbance around their houses during the day that usually intensify with the advent of the dark. Some report perpetually sensing a presence outside their house, either due to the sounds these intruders make, the moving shadows, or alarm installations going off. Sometimes they only know someone is out there by feeling the actual sensation from an attack launched on them. There are those cases, especially where the target is a woman, when entry into the premises is forced while they are in the house, especially when asleep, waking up to find total strangers standing in their bedroom.

Some of these occurrences may seem unreal to those who live in a secure world where the only place this is expected is in the movies, especially the horror, crime or science fiction genres. It is only when you make people see how much space is created in our individualistic life styles for such events to occur that they begin to see the possibility of it happening to them or someone they know. Only when you show how vulnerable our own lives are to such attacks, how easy it would be for an immoral, often psychotic person to isolate an unsuspecting individual if they so wish, then proceed to haunt that life in abnormal, indescribable manners, with impunity; in part to eliminate the victim, but evidently also to feed a psychotic addiction, do we start to believe these stories, which for most of us will unfortunately come too late.

Some TI's are lucky in that they have at one time or another caught their tormentors red-handed. Some have caught them in the act of sabotage, or have recorded instances of abnormal harassment or surveillance on camera. They have as such provided themselves and others with real evidence of the activity; have assured themselves they are not making things up.

The vast majority, however, are not as lucky, and remain trapped in an unreal world where mature men and women can go to insane lengths to get a single thing done, for example speeding up ahead of a target when they discover where he/she is headed so that they can crowd the checkout line, or working shifts in the houses next to the target just so that they can replicate activities, or report when he/she takes out the trash.

No matter how many measures targets take or threats they make against these people, no matter how many times they attempt to catch at least one instance of a figure engaged in attack activities, the stalkers keep evading, mostly coming back with ever more outrageousness the next time around.

Under such circumstances, it is easy for a target to start doubting their sanity, to start believing they suffer from paranoia or are delusional. Knowledge heat sensitive devices and other technologies exist that can allow people to see through walls, some of it so simple it can be handheld, can provide for some needed reprieve from negative thoughts as it goes a long way in explaining why these people are so elusive.

If they can watch the target and neighbors from within the four walls of their house, then they can easily know when best to attack. This means they only make a move on the house when they know the target is involved in activities that encumber the speed with which they can react to a noise outside, if they were to hear something.

But then it takes an adult with extraordinary beliefs not to wait hours for that moment to come when the coast is clear enough to take the expensive car away, but to go over to the front door of a house and plant a stink bomb; to wait for hours on end for a sound to come from the house next door so they can mimic it, to wait for a target to flush the toilet just so they can honk a horn, to wait for the target to take a shower so they can do the same; to wait, then run out of their house so they can make a rude gesture or hurl obscenities when the target goes out to throw the trash; to wait for there to be signs the target is going out so that they can warn other people, who will take turns and shifts following the target so they in their turn can contribute that little nuisance to the target's day.

The absurdity surrounding such activities, especially the fact most members show a lack of individual identity, is the reason most people believe such groups are far from everyday people, but cult members who are working for an agenda.

Closer scrutiny of the average stalker reveals there's something much simpler than ideology controlling their actions, something that lies within the depths of their own minds, and also shows that their actions only seem abnormal to outsiders to such activities, because the gangs always know exactly what they are doing. This is also revealed in many statements made by targeted individuals, and also in the reality targets are not always walkovers.

Targets come in all shapes, sizes and sexes. It can be expected that the females are easy pickings because of their softer nature. Stalkers are then unlikely to come up against personalities capable of being a threat to their own physical health. But then the majority of targets are males, mostly in their prime, among whom are those who have enough connections within their community, and can rally these against such gangs, who are not only capable of aggression, but are roused enough, as it were, to act out the aggression if they identify a stalker. There are undoubtedly a lot of people who are not going to take such abuse lying down and others who are already under attack who have made it very plain they will retaliate once they catch even one single stalker in the act. Yet the stalkers keep coming back even in cases where their very lives are potentially threatened.

Perpetrators of covert warfare are in fact perfect Manchurian Candidates, the best dreams of MKULTRA and similar programs, because they are actual, programmed devices that will act in a given way when a switch is pulled. They are fearless because they are taking a choice between two evils, in which the chance of suffering injury from the target or his connections is the lesser. They are disciplined because they are under pressure that they feel to an extreme degree due to the parameters of their minds that also accounts for their personalities and their fear of consequences if they fail to carry out directives.

Think of them as an army of individuals who have been sentenced through the legal judicial system to die for various, depraved crimes, but are given a chance at freedom if they carry out a given mission.

It is actually so easy to create a Manchurian Candidate most people will not believe this only on account of the simplicity involved, especially since the majority are inclined towards the belief it takes highly complex procedures to achieve a sleeper state in a human being.

It is really the effect of individual mental limitations, and favors or privileges candidates for the role are given that combine to have the eventual and real effect of turning otherwise healthy persons into zombies carrying out orders, zombies that nonetheless attend meticulously to detail; who can lie in wait for hours on end, waiting for that singular sound from a singular person to which they have to act in a certain way, aimed at creating or preventing a specific state in the victim; machines that can even marry the target, or into the target's family, only to lie in wait then carry out the act they were programmed to do at a time when their handlers so desire, when the switch is pulled, which can come years after recruitment. The state of their minds is also almost always a result of covert attacks, including psychological manipulations they are subjected to themselves that result in negative feedback loops aimed at maintaining the negative personality, that ensure they exist in a more or less vegetative state throughout. It makes them easier to predict, while also making them safe to handle.

Many may argue that the high level of discipline gang members display, if it can be called that, is purely a consequence of the military style training they are believed to receive, which is known to achieve the same results with military recruits so that they are able to carry out any mission on command. Though there are a lot of issues about the methods employed in military training, the military is a legal institution in society, whose legality extends to war situations; no matter how unjustified the war itself is; whereas there is no legality attached to the activity of launching covert warfare on innocent civilians. Citizen harassment and elimination groups can as such not comprise entirely of people drilled into an obedient state from scratch, in the same manner military recruits are, as this has the potential to affect not only the potency, but especially the secrecy of their activities. Incidences of desertion are common in militaries, and have measured though non-disastrous effects, whereas the same could have dire consequences for a gang of criminals such as citizen stalkers.

This is the reason the vast majority, and arguably those who come closest to figures in authority, consist of people who are so deep in depravity, criminal activity or other activities with the potential to restrain their freedom to the extent they would not have anywhere to run if they had a change of conscience, since society would reject, if not punish them more severely than their handlers ever could.

It is not even every deviant or criminal who would fit the profile of the average member. Strong willed individuals who know what they are doing when they commit a crime, and are prepared for the punishment society will mete out, are not a very good candidate for the role. These individuals will always follow their own convictions, and would as such form a risk element in such gangs as they could easily reveal what they know, and be fully prepared for the consequences.

Persons who live dangerously without being aware, who end up as a consequence of this lifestyle in a situation they didn't really consider a potential outcome of the behavior; such as when they cannot face up to the prospect of life imprisonment, are the kind recruiters would be looking out for, and they will be approached at the opportune moment of coming to terms with such a fate, when desperation is at its height. Persons with the potential to unnecessarily complicate their own situation, those who will misinterpret signs they see, and end up accumulating more wrongs as they go along, especially those who have already accrued hideous secrets that makes them potential targets of violence in any society they may live as a result of this propensity to walk into walls, are best suited for recruitment.

These people could include habitual offenders, violent criminals, others whose crimes are a result of an addiction, even a deviancy society doesn't tolerate, such as paedophiles, rapists, serial murderers, etc. The list does not need to end with such extreme cases, but could go on to include any person who can be blackmailed on account of a colossal personality flaw. It could also include asylum seekers or illegal persons whose worst nightmare is deportation. Basically, it is anyone who can be made to do anything on account of a deep seated fear.

I once had the opportunity to get acquainted with a neighbor who would later go on to be recruited by a group pursuing me. He tried his level best to have me understand, by indirect statements made whenever opportunity gave, that he was given little choice in this, believing I would forgive his weakness if I put myself in his shoes. According to him, he would either have been deported on account of the reality he was illegal, or would have ended up homeless, with his capacity to get a job permanently curtailed.

He made it plain he had not had problems prior to the time I appeared on the scene, after which he started feeling his life would only improve if I left. He was a neighbor who lived a few doors away from my flat, but his very existence became that much more of a nightmare than mine since I could more or less insulate myself from the stalker world for given lengths of time, whereas his existence became tied to how well he performed regarding my case. If, for example, I were to leave the premises without him informing the group, he would get attacked where he felt it most, making it necessary that he constantly keep his eyes on my door.

Most people who have been used once go on to be used for other missions, mostly on the same threats since the stalking groups already know their weaknesses. They get used in the same or other location, accruing as much complicity along the way as would make it almost impossible to reject further requests, driving them further away from redemption. The rationalization presented by my neighbor for his decision to join makes sense only to a man with a very limited imagination, with bigger than life fears. Accepting to do the dirty work eventually puts him in more trouble than he could ever have imagined.

I was actually already aware of recruitment activities prior to meeting this neighbor. I know that the process goes hand in hand with defamation campaigns against a TI; situations where the victim is made highly visible to a fault in society, and know of many more people who revealed they had been approached, who refused to accept or comply with requests. In most instances, these people would quickly move away from the area as they too would become targets of harassment.

The suitability of a particular individual for a given case is crucial. A member of a racist, right wing extremist organization would be best suited for a non-racist white person, also called a bleeding heart, an African or homosexual target as he could be trusted to do a good job against an individual he is told poses a real and imminent threat to the white race or white supremacy, and should be punished in the worst way possible. A homosexual on the other hand would be perfectly suited for a campaign against the same right wing extremist whom he recognizes as his worst enemy.

An African criminal with a rape conviction who is released early and kept anonymous in the community, where he is manoeuvred into setting up a lucrative drug running business, will be suitable for any mission whatsoever on account of his gratitude for the early release and anonymous stature, and the false sense of being above the law that his handlers would eventually foster in him. Such a person could come to literary feel complicity with crimes committed by those who give him odd jobs now and then. He could work well against or alongside the extremist, against the homosexual or an African man, with or without a good reason.

Recruits are approached from anywhere: on the streets, places of work, while they are in prison, but especially when there is a target against whom they can easily be rallied in the neighborhood, an object that's deliberately been made highly visible to a fault, upon whom they can direct their hate. The last method of recruitment is the most used because it has immediate and lasting psychological impact. They are either directly given the proposal, or put through a succession of trials to ascertain their suitability for stalking roles. For example, an offender can be freed unexpectedly from prison, then followed through until they have re- offended, then approached with an either-or proposal.

I have not come across information that indicates they are put through a ritual of initiation similar to that which cult members are known to undergo, but the fact some of them were targets of harassment similar to that which targets experience suggests it could very well be the case.

Once they are full members however, it is an established fact authority deliberately turns a blind eye to offences they may commit, but not without putting these on the record for the purpose of blackmail. These new recruits are made aware with their every waking hour that everything they do can be used against them and their only hope of staying free and enjoying the freedom is to obey, to work hard, which in the case of covert warfare on innocent civilians can sometimes mean doing the abnormal.

Turning a blind eye to crimes some of these individuals are prone to commit has the potential of instilling a false sense of power in them, a sense of being above the law, as David Lawson, author of "Terrorist Stalking in America", also notes. Many may foolishly go on a crime rampage knowing no retribution shall be forthcoming, increasing the level to which they become entangled in blackmail as everything they do will be held against them by their handlers. In cases where monetary rewards are involved, for example drug dealing or such, the freedom may give the individual false hope the activity will provide them with the ticket to more power.

The efforts of those pulling the strings are however concentrated on keeping the recruits stuck in the same position. When a gang member starts getting too big, they are quickly cut down to size. It is very common in the stalking world for members to suddenly disappear behind bars for some time, especially around moments when they have reaped substantial successes in illegal dealings. There are those times when entry into prison is a call of duty, but others were they are actually serving time.

From some statements I heard from many stalkers, a deep-seated belief remains that it is impossible to escape without being found, wherever in the world they may run to. Among members, examples abound of cases where an individual tried to escape but was found, and brought back to face "justice".

I learnt of the realities I divulge above by talking to actual stalkers when they would say things that revealed more than they could possibly conceive, and also while listening to conversations between people I identified as members of stalking gangs, who did not know I had the capacity to critically analyze their statements and reach viable conclusions; or through people who were not directly involved, but would unconsciously get inside knowledge because they happened to be close friends of a stalker and knew facts about their lives that only such close friendship allows, who would inadvertently reveal the secrets this world keeps hidden by what they said about the life or fate of a friend who had suddenly disappeared, for example.

Organization: Hierarchy and Connections

According to David Lawson,

> *Stalking groups do not hold traditional meetings. They meet by cell phone when they are in their vehicles. Following and harassing various targets is part of their daily activities when they are on patrol. In order to avoid potential destruction of their groups, they use a concept which has been used by political and paramilitary groups for hundreds of years. A name currently used by right wing organizations is "leaderless resistance".*

> *Leaderless resistance is used in an attempt to isolate group leaders from prosecution, while allowing their followers an unlimited operational range. Leaders identify targets to their followers through broadcasts on right wing radio stations, in print articles, or on web sites, but they never tell their followers what to do. It is up to them to decide what action is appropriate.*

Stalkers arrange their activities so that they protect their leaders from prosecution, at the same time protecting the whole group. This means most of them do not actually know, nor have they met their leaders, nor do they know who in particular is giving a specific directive. They therefore answer to a hooded party, hooded for the purpose of preventing identification since they are not willing to stand up for, let alone face what they do.

The hooded party functions as judge and jury and comprises highly placed individuals taking up key positions in society, mostly in government or law enforcement. The executioners, those who carry out the elimination of the targets, who in most cases are either lied to about the reason the person has been turned in for harassment or elimination, who carry out such orders for crumbs, favors and handouts, comprise the average, everyday citizen. Outwardly, these people are not cut from a particular social cloth, but can include doctors, lawyers, menial laborers, the homeless, etc. Many are considered upright, though in reality they may not really know right from wrong.

The punishment this last group metes out comes in the form of covert attacks on unsuspecting citizens that are as brutal and relentless as they are systematic and sophisticated; in most cases known to last for the natural life of the victims. Some victims commit suicide, most go through life not knowing what, who or why they were targeted.

Beware of an ongoing campaign to deceive the general public, specifically the tendency for a lot of information on the subject of covert warfare to focus solely on those attacks whose motivation can be considered trivial enough to lean towards the innocuous. This is done in order to dissociate in the mind direct involvement by higher authority, especially government, law enforcement or citizen organizations. This avoidance of the establishmentarian is aimed at eventually limiting the phenomena to cult groups, low esteem or retarded individuals, disgruntled citizens, xenophobes, extremists, overzealous believers, ill-informed neighborhood-watch, vigilante justice, or racists.

By so saying, I do not want to imply every government official or police officer is involved. Indeed, many are oblivious of this reality, but then as many of these officials are involved as would make each organization completely corrupted in this way.

Overwhelming evidence clearly shows the sinister, most wide spread variant of citizen harassment is done with the involvement of higher authority, meaning government. In fact, this connection forms the most potent form of this harassment, the most widespread, the most likely to happen to anybody. This is easily proven without need for complex supporting arguments.

It is the sheer scope of such activities, the numbers of people involved, the resources and technology at their disposal, that is also displayed openly by members of such groups; the lengths of time victims are followed, but especially the impunity with which some of these activities are carried out; more especially the concerted hushing up or lack of interest and disbelief shown by those who have the power to either inform the public (media), or put an end to the covert torture (authority), that exposes the truth this is far from being solely an exercise by deranged, deluded or retarded minds.

When you live in areas where the most subtly carried out crime can be investigated and, from a few clues left by the perpetrator(s), solved, then broadcast over the airwaves, where, for example, even more subtle methods of smuggling illegal goods can be uncovered, and the criminals prosecuted; you know something is wrong when crimes that are much more visible to law enforcement go unpunished. When you live in areas where camera surveillance equipment is installed at every corner, it is hard, in fact impossible to believe that a group of individuals as noisy and indiscrete to authority as stalkers are known to be can get away with the kind of illegal activities they engage in.

Though they may not hold traditional meetings, citizen harassment groups have been observed, in fact it is known they make a habit of congregating in large groups; in near endless convoys of cars, for example. It is known that when a target has been turned in for harassment, the location where the victim lives usually becomes a high traffic area, burglaries become more frequent, drug dealing sometimes goes on the rise (as authority turns a blind eye to illegal activities of members of the gangs as a favor to them), etc. It may not be possible for the average civilian to make sense of such activities, but then not for authority that has a wider view of any given area in society. These activities have as much potential to attract attention from these circles as meetings would, especially since most gang activity is done out of necessity, therefore concomitant to every single case.

For example, gang members have to move in and out of accommodation in order to keep as close to their victims as possible; by necessity crossing with neighborhood watches set up to detect suspicious activity; who under normal circumstances should be made aware of the intimidation necessary for the aiding and abetting that is known to accompany the activities. This includes neighbors who are forced to cooperate with operations, or keep their mouths shut; landlords who give them the abode that affords strategic positioning with regards the target. These people are known to be recruiting even more people into their gangs as they go along, an expansion itself that involves a lot of exposure, making the keeping of their little secret impossible. They are known to control traffic and other lights, changing these at will to unnerve targets, or impress new members; they are known to cause visible traffic congestion, use high intensity Directed Energy Weapons (DEW) without fear the beams can be detected by anyone with the equipment.

They may disorient and cause the target to look insane or sick to unsuspecting others, thus succeeding to isolate him/her; they may use all manner of tricks to make some people believe the victim brought his suffering on him/herself, but then all of the activities that affect such a state cannot fool all of the people all the time because they require a lot of free mingling with a diverse public in the immediate neighborhood; a lot of conversing, shaking of hands, giving of names, paying of money, sharing of meals or drinks, intimidation or other forms of exposure.

A lot of the members of such groups are known to join out of fear of what would happen to them otherwise, which implies a cowardly nature. Some join out of warped beliefs or misplaced hate, revealing a lack of general intelligence. Many are known to join or carry out directives for crumby handouts and favors, showing a general lack of resourcefulness. They are known to fall for any reason given for a person's elimination, meaning they are a gullible bunch. When these and many more negative personality traits are considered, we can conclude the majority members constitute the average noisy bum that is easily led by the nose, and cannot possibly be nondescript by juxtaposition with such extraordinary activities. In individual members, especially those who actually directly intimidate locals or take up accommodation, there must surely be a trail of evidence that should easily follow them through wherever they go, and eventually lead to their leaders.

This, of course, is what would happen in an ideal world. This would be the case if authorities in a given country were really interested in putting an end to this form of terrorism.

The fact remains these mentally challenged warriors are carrying out the dirty end of the status quo retention game. They are the prison warders and executioners in a new kind of concentration camp that is not fixed of location; the streets and homes serving as holding pens and gas chambers, with the added function of spectator areas.

They are the employees in a parallel justice system that those who have infiltrated authority believe is essential to maintaining order as they want it to be, hence the reality their duty is to persecute people whose deeds cannot be faulted under existing, socially sanctioned laws. They are an illegal part of the system, given the nod, wherewithal, and acknowledged indirectly by their members in authority, and this accounts for the impunity with which they can carry out operations that would otherwise be too noisy for authority not to hear.

The fault here is therefore not a hypocritical society shying away from confronting its uncanny excesses, its darker appetites; or individuals within that society who are too frightened to confront this monstrosity, but those entrusted with authority feeling and knowing existing laws cannot guarantee their hold on power, and as such the agendas they have.

I must make it clear again, before going on, that I am not anti law enforcement or anti government, but anti corruption in these institutions. A lot of evidence suggests the average policeman or civil servant, even bureaucrat who has become a denizen in such an institution through the process of "bureaucratic capture", doesn't know of the existence of such groups. There are a lot of people in government and law enforcement who are conscientious, who do the right thing. There are police officers who have testified being targets of such gangs, targeted because they are outspoken on issues only the leaders of such groups know are sacrosanct. This in itself does not exempt the existence of bad apples within these social institutions, or the possibility the corruption has completely changed their intended purpose in society.

Testimony from people who have infiltrated the lower end of the gangs, the executioners, or members of law enforcement who are not involved, most speaking under condition of anonymity, supports this last statement.

It isn't even the case that law enforcement has still to get its head around this problem because it is new. Citizen harassment, as indeed tests and abuse, including pedophilia under the guise of research in the case of the infamous Nazi Dr. Josef Mengeles's MKULTRA experiments, on suspecting citizens by those who are supposed to be looking out for their best interests, has been going on in especially developed countries for a long time now. Experiences of attacks were until recently private affairs, and are only coming to the general public's attention because of the internet revolution where information sharing has enabled people from all walks of life, races, nations and cultures, who would otherwise have conveniently been isolated, to identify similar events in others, and relate experiences and recommend manners of coping.

Random online surveys carried out in the USA and several European countries revealed a staggering average of 1 individual in every 100 has at one time or over a prolonged period been a victim of such attacks. This is easily 10 thousand in an average city.

Corporations may harass those they want silenced, and scorned spouses may seek revenge by hiring gangs to make hell out of the other's life. Extremist right wing organizations may employ such methods against minorities, but all of these activities are limited in scope and, especially in the case of corporations and whistleblowers, are occurrences that cease as soon as the target, who is a single individual, has been silenced or discredited. They are limited in scope in the majority of the other cases thanks to meager budgets and limited access to the necessary resources. They could not possibly account for the prevalence and ever expanding nature of the phenomenon in modern day societies.

Institutionalization of Covert Warfare

Because covert citizen harassment and elimination has become so extensive and commonplace in so many disparate cultures, even in the "third world", the political motive alone appears to be the major reason as to why such an expensive network of citizen harassers came about.

In their formative years, dictatorships are known to use similar methods to win elections, and once they are in power, the very same methods ensure the government stays in control. In this sense, the covert harassment and elimination of citizens who pose a threat to those in power becomes a way of life once the dictatorship has been established. It becomes institutionalized, which means it is not only entrenched in the system, an identifiable aspect of it, but an activity vital to the functioning of the system itself.

The phenomenon of citizen harassment and elimination we are seeing in our day is not exclusive to our times. It has been identified for as long as the present system has lasted. It was handed down from the past where it became as integral to the system as the visible judicial system that it runs parallel to, in what is an inevitable outcome.

Traditionally, it is the duty of every intelligence agency to keep ahead of foreign, as well as internal threats to national cohesion. Only when threats to the government come from citizens of a given country who are subject to the laws that govern the land, and these activities have not broken any of these laws, does there arise a situation when extra-judicial measures become necessary to curb the threat. It is when the judicial system fails to serve a dictatorship's needs, and laws preventing the activities that threaten the government's hold on power cannot be passed because they would be considered repressive, that the agency that is supposed to protect a people against real external and internal threats is called in to become the agency that protects the government from its own citizens, even when they have not broken any laws.

Such a culmination eventually leads to a situation where certain truths have to be suppressed or altered for fear they will cause outrage in the populace at large. This could include murders committed by men in authority against citizens or other people in authority who had done no wrong, or policies that caused suffering of untold proportions to segments of society or other countries. Keeping ugly truths buried requires misinformation campaigns, the deliberate instilling of ignorance in schools so that an average intelligence level is effected that finds arriving at answers too demanding; deliberate manipulation of lifestyles so a sense of complicity in atrocities committed by a government is fostered in as many people as is possible; murder of those who discover some truths, etc.

This conniving creates rows of wrongs to answer for and, considering the dynamic nature of society, perpetually gives rise to situations where each wrong in turn calls for more wrongs to cover up. Rather than create a situation where differences are finally settled, more and more work is instead required to keep this past buried. With the rise in number of atrocities against members of a community also rises the level of potential outrage, so that the entirety of the population increasingly becomes the greatest enemy that the government becomes wary of, that it has to be protected from.

Modern demands of intelligence gathering usually require that a significant number of employees be people who are not only highly educated, have worldly knowledge, but are also intelligent; if they are expected to make sense of the data gathered by their officers in real life, highly complex situations. Those who are mediocre of mind are reliable in a dictatorship not only because they cannot tell the difference between right and wrong, but also because they do not have what it takes to make anything out of what they might learn. Such people can not only be trusted to carry out orders that might evidently be against their own good, but are incapable of posing a threat to those in power whatever they may learn as they go along.

But then only a government lacking ambition will rely entirely for its intelligence gathering on an endless abyss of poodles, as these could easily misinterpret facts, fail to take appropriate measures in response to real threats. They could fail to read from the signs of the times impeding disaster, or fail to innovate when necessary. Preventing the agency being prone to potentially catastrophic lapses in judgment necessitates the recruitment of individuals who are mental gurus of sorts to work alongside the crowd of poodles.

This creates a situation where workers within this organ be people who could eventually pose some kind of threat to leadership, who are by virtue of their intellectual capacities unsuitable for campaigns that threaten their numbers in society, those that are the agency's responsibility; such as those that require the increase in the level of ignorance in society, official malfeasance, and gratuitous attacks on innocent civilians, covert biological and chemical attacks capable of backfiring on society itself, etc. Whistleblowers or others who can work from within the system to change negative orientations are usually enlightened people, in most cases exposed to information that forces them to make the choice between silence and guaranteed catastrophe, or action and possible correction.

The agency itself would require expansion to be able to cope with such a campaign, without mentioning the expense of such a project calculated from such expansion and salaries to cope with the increase in workers, or the backlash for the agency when the conspiracy is uncovered. Part time workers who are not associated with the agency, consisting mainly of upright but shallow civilians active as vigilantes or neighborhood watch; capable of carrying out, without question, any given task, not on a high salary but for handouts or favors; who are given the equipment and leadership they need by a corrupted wing of the intelligence agency, becomes the best option.

Out of this should subsequently be born an army, a standing one of sorts, that's actively watching out and eliminating those who are a threat to a given order or the government behind the order, which by necessity must be ever expanding.

Covert warfare on civilians is a powerful way of controlling populations at large, because it keeps them embracing the illusion they are a free people, especially since it rids the populace of those who would remind them otherwise, those who have found out truths hidden from the general population through hard work or research. It keeps the population at large believing in their government, ensured this organ has done them no wrong, even going to the extent of believing individuals who incur the wrath of gangs that wage covert warfare, that some people are very aware exist in society, are in fact a threat to the whole. It keeps people believing they are equal players, non-expendable participants in the affairs of their country who cannot at any moment be sacrificed for the interests of a few.

The point of covert warfare is to avoid overt shows of violence that reveal to the masses the oppression they live under, and force them to protect themselves. This is easily shown in the pattern of attacks, more especially the profile of people who get attacked. This should be self evident from the fact there is something very wrong with a corporation or government covertly silencing a whistleblower or activist when society already has structures designed to prosecute those in the wrong, especially those who pose a threat to it, which can be amended or appended as new information becomes available. This avoidance of the normal channels for such procedures clearly points to wrongdoing.

The number of times influential people can be killed in accidents or in encounters with madmen without raising eyebrows is limited. When individuals, who are friends, spouses, parents, loved in the community at large, cross some hidden line, their continual and overt elimination is sooner or later likely to backfire on the government. Means of elimination of opposition that leave no signs foul play is involved, least of all that someone out there has ungodly plans for the community, minorities, or others outside the national borders, is the better method of solving such problems.

Chapter 3
What are The Attack Methods?

In This Chapter
▶ Psychological Harassment
▶ Direct Physical Violence

The methods employed in covert attacks are varied, and mostly case specific, but they all share the objective of complete isolation of the victim before elimination. Once the TI has been isolated, the stalkers ensure that the victim gets round the clock surveillance that can even include through the wall observation accompanied by attempts to make the victim aware his every move within the privacy of his home is being observed, achieved by for example making the same sounds whenever the TI engages in certain activities. This is pure attrition, meant to drive the victim to breaking point.

Psychological Harassment

There are times when a TI is driven to isolation; to the belief they are delusional, or even led to suicide without the actual use of poisons or weapons that damage any part of their body, but by pure psychological manipulation alone. The likelihood for this outcome depends in large part on the victim's imagination.

A person who can not phantom the possibility several people can be recruited to stand at intervals along a given path so they can say something to them, is easy to convince they are fantasizing. Likewise, a person who would never imagine the sudden rise in the number of cars in the neighborhood could be deliberate, only on account of the given person's inability to conceive of the possibility there could be a group capable of mobilizing as many people in as many cars; a target who for the same reason would think he is hearing things when strangers start divulging information that is private to them, can easily be led into believing they are delusional.

Any person who believes they, as a singular individual, would never be worthy of the kind of attention described here does not understand how the politics of covert warfare work, and is as such prone to fall into the same trap. Anybody who would not believe that corporations or governments will go to the extent of hiring a gang of criminals to corner an individual in ways described here, to spy and replicate their movements within their own homes, even go to the extent of breaking in and moving furniture around to undermine them psychologically, would very easily end up on medications for a mental disorder such as schizophrenia.

The tactics used in this psychological warfare are as many as the stalkers can come up with. There is however one approach that is strictly adhered to in all cases. This is the "inside-out" method of attack. The first part of the attack's objective is the destruction of the TI's personality. The point of starting at this level is to ensure a TI's personality is demolished to the extent they can not counter the attack at any other level to which it is taken. Once this is achieved, the show then moves on to include the greater world of the victim, such as relatives and occupational relationships. Opinions of relatives and other acquaintances are directly or indirectly influenced against the target, in manners they find hard to defend against, ensuring his/her isolation.

The stalkers make sure they do those things to a target that would seem normal when related to other people, so that eventually, even in cases where the TI is aware he/she is under attack, they inevitably end up alone in this experience.

Meeting several people on a day out who are extremely rude or insulting is not a normal, every day occurrence, but if a target was to try and relate this experience to another person, then the impression they would usually get from this is there is something wrong with either the individual's behavior in public that is attracting negative reactions, or that they are imagining things.

If a target were to relate that he/she believes his/her room is being entered because things do not seem to be in the places where they were left, but nothing is ever stolen, then those hearing this will most probably suspect a mental problem, or paranoia in the individual telling the story, since they could not imagine why anybody would break into a house for the purpose of shifting objects around. As said already, how others respond to the realities a target will relate is dependent on their imagination.

It is also dependent on the way other people know the individual relating the story. Usually, without even being aware of this, a lot of people tend to attach value to personalities. Hearing accounts of this nature forces them to calculate whether the value they have attached to the individual is worth the attacks they are relating, and in most cases, again according to imagination, they come to the conclusion that it isn't.

There are a lot of men and women on serious medication for schizophrenia who in actual fact have become mentally ill due to the medications they have been led to believe will help them, who landed in mental institutions due to intense psychological attacks of the kind described here, involving the crowding out of a TI's life in perpetual staged encounters designed to give the victim an impression of self or reality that is not in accordance with the truth. These campaigns are subtle, calculated, and carried out with professional accuracy. They are so relentless and intense that, unless the target comes to the realization they are under attack by an unknown party, the effect will be to leave little doubt in the TI's mind the staged reality is the truth itself.

In Holland, I was fortunate enough to meet and talk to a few people on medication for mental disorders who related extreme occurrences such as hearing voices, meeting people on the streets who knew what could not possibly be known about their private lives, or that they thought the television screen was telling stories too particular to things that had happened in their own lives, so that they would believe someone was trying to talk to them alone, out of the millions of viewers out there.

Of course, all of this sounds insane for the simple fact it is impossible, but then if we ignore the diagnosis made by the man in a white coat and investigate the delusion, we discover some truths with some of these tales that might make us change our mind about the initial state of the patient's mind. We might even discover how much of the paranoid delusion is latent or induced.

Some of the acts necessary to create the stories are actually not beyond the capacities of individuals within society to carry out. This means that, given sufficient motivation, there are people in society with the contacts and resources to pull off some of the deception necessary to drive a select individual to believe they are insane. The opinion of society on this issue will obviously be against the individual relating such experiences because, as far as most people are concerned, such things just don't happen.

I do not want to give the impression I believe all people in mental institutions are not sick. There are people who have mental problems, as the spiritual and physical nature of the mind makes the apparatus prone to damage and flaws that could result in various malfunctions, some of which can manifest as schizophrenia. The fact remains that some stories told by mental cases are too similar to those told by people who had strong enough personalities to resist psychological harassment, especially those who are known to have gone on to provide recorded and written evidence of this form of terrorism. There is clear evidence psychological warfare exists that is capable of convincing an unwitting person they are insane. Some people have survived such attacks, while others have definitely fallen. There is here the real possibility that when we see some mental cases, we are in actual fact confronted with cases of people who fell to psychological warfare.

The 1944 Hollywood movie "Gaslight", in which Charles Boyer tries to convince his wife that she's going insane by contriving incidents designed to make it appear she's forgetful, disoriented, and confused, provides a small scale version of how the process works. In the movie, Boyer is a singular individual playing mind games on his wife so that he can convince her she is delusional, whereas in real life situations it is a group of individuals who outnumber the victim, capable of mobile communication and as such coordinating their activities, capable of creating a complete web around the victim. Outnumbered and outdone, few people can successfully fight off such invasions into their private lives.

This method of covert attack is sometimes called "gaslighting", after the same film. The book "Gaslighting - How to Drive Your Enemies Crazy" by Victor Santoro, is a very good place to start for anyone who wants to familiarize themselves with the details of the method.

Direct Physical Violence

This method combines psychological harassment with direct physical violence, that can be perpetrated on the target, next of kin, sometimes against children of the TI by children of stalkers in school. A lot of sabotage of personal property may be involved, and lethal attacks on pets are sometimes known to go on to murder of close relatives.

In cases where the stalkers cannot get into the victim's house at all, or regularly enough, they will move their attacks to objects the individual uses but leaves outside, including those the TI merely touches, and places the individual frequents. The door knob, air inlets of cars, seats and handlebars of bicycles and motorcycles can be sprayed or smeared with all manner of toxic substances, to be inhaled or absorbed into the body.

Pubs, gyms, churches, even public transportation will be occupied by the stalkers before the victim even arrives or boards, who will then take every opportunity possible to get as close to the target as would enable them to unleash some form of attack, that can sometimes be airborne if the stalkers have not predicted the victim's favorite sitting place.

Attacks with hazardous chemicals or biological agents are not as rare as many would believe. Their widespread use accounts for the worn down and zombie like state in which most members of such gangs are reported to be, and not always a result of the drug abuse they are known to engage in. What usually happens is they are told how to use these agents, but then, like they are lied to about everything else, are not told of the real risks, so that they do not give themselves sufficient protection.

In supermarkets, articles of shopping can be swapped with contaminated ones. This is done in shopping baskets or wagons while the subject is not looking, or on the shelf itself so that the victim picks up the product intended for him/her.

It is crucial to understand here that all of this is possible because of the time the stalkers, for whom this is a way of life, have on their hands to study the habits of their victim. They also possess the means to move ahead of the TI, using the advantage of numbers and mobile phones to communicate, placing a few individuals in locations the victim frequents, ensuring a constant net around the victim all the time.

These attacks are also known to involve Directed Energy Weapons. DEW's are classified or unclassified electronic devises with potentially lethal consequences that utilize either electro magnetic fields or various radio frequencies, of which are microwave frequencies, to do harm to the victim. This can include the inducing of disease, control of mood, or the destruction of organs, including the brains of targeted individuals.

Because such weapons can go through walls, stalkers do not need to enter the property of the victim. If they have managed to secure accommodation next to the victim, then they will use electronic devices to observe and target the individual from their location, otherwise they carry the device in a vehicle that they then park as close to the target's residence as they can.

DEW's are the weapon of choice of such gangs of criminals because of their capacity to be deployed remotely, and also because they leave no sign foul play is involved when the victim starts exhibiting symptoms of disease or dies. Among the many known effects, they can cause sleep deprivation or malaise in the targeted individual. Some people have reported sterility when especially their genitals were the favorite target of the waves emanating from such weapons, while others are known to have developed cancers.

They can instill fear, rage, tetanize muscles, cause heart attacks, memory loss, cancer, and are also known to manipulate hormones. When used over a prolonged period, they can cause a wide variety of illnesses, including lupus, fibro-myalgia, multiple sclerosis, chronic fatigue, lymphatic breakdown, depressed immune system, low t-cell count, etc.

Chapter 4

Why people become targets of covert warfare

In This Chapter
▶ pre-emptive Strategy: Potential Threat Elimination
▶ Mentacide: Deliberate Destruction of the Mind
▶ Relational and Other Problems
▶ Xenophobic and Racial
▶ Political and Economic

It's important to keep in mind anyone can become a victim. A lot of the members of gangs of citizen harassers have themselves at one time or another been victims of this form of covert warfare. Some joined 'willingly', but only because, at some point in the process of harassment, their spirit was broken. In so saying, I do not wish to provide extenuation for the activities these individuals engage in, but then we can agree if it can be proven an element of force was involved in their recruitment, then there are people who are attacked who weren't necessarily active in ways that traditionally engender attacks of this nature, nor could such people have found their way to the front door of such groups by themselves. They were targeted because they may have been considered useful in ways only members of such gangs can know.

Pre-Emptive Strategy: Potential Threat Elimination

There are a lot of people chosen because they are vulnerable, especially people isolated from society for various reasons, who get targeted for recruitment, or training purposes. We can progress up this ladder to the point where good reasons exist as to why people are targeted, for example whistleblowers and activists, but between these and the previous group are a whole lot of people who could potentially face covert attacks for reasons that are unknown, or too trivial to be considered as such.

For example, some people are targeted because they have the potential to pose a threat to authority, not because they are already a threat. This means they have not done anything yet, may not even be mature adults, and are not consciously against a given order even if statements they tend to make may imply this. They may not have amassed the knowledge necessary to be a threat to anybody yet. This would include people who are naturally bright, who are headstrong and believe they have all the right answers even though instilled. They could be people nurtured to be on the side of the underdog, people who are inclined as such to be tuned into this source of information, and still others easily taken by underdog points of view. They could be responding to peer pressure, or merely acting out roles that are not in line with the interests of some people in power. They may be charismatic and not know it, be influential to the opinions of their peers in manners that could potentially be against some hidden agendas.

We are talking here of people who are vociferous on economic and political issues, who may be pertinacious in their beliefs rather than flexible, who are active members of society, engaging in debates on issues that touch on core causes, whose precocious abilities to make sense out of chaos illuminates vague issues for others. These people may not be active members of organizations that stand at loggerheads with authority where certain policy is concerned, but are as likely to become victims of covert attacks as those who are members, and only because of their inert nature.

Society has long since reached a point where those in authority wait for individuals to become a real threat to them before they act. The new pre-emptive strategy has become part and parcel of how such culminations are avoided; irregardless records show a lot of innocent victims are claimed along the way. Intelligence agencies that are ambitious no longer merely react to perceived threats. This means the process of detecting enemy activity goes hand in hand with that of preventing it and, as has been observed with imperialistic countries in our time, the process of artificially creating threats in order to rally the masses behind a cause. It includes overt surveillance, intimidation, attrition, and elimination; operations designed as much for pre-emptive incapacitation as examples for deterrence.

There are those things foreigners, secret agent or civilian, just can't do in some countries, that the host country's leaders make very clear once the line is crossed. These realities are never bluntly spelt out, so that they constitute actual webs in which a lot of people will inevitably get ensnared. Governments avoid revealing these hidden lines because they are fearful this could drive local residents or potential immigrants away, especially those with the potential to contribute positively to the welfare of the country. Within these lines would be writ large how oppressive or paranoid a society is, making the dangers an individual could face in that society clear.

I was once shopping at a market in Brest, a southern border Belarus city in the former Soviet Union. Everything was going smoothly until I asked where I could buy a map of the city. The owner of the souvenir shop, obviously a connected fellow, loudly repeated my request, bringing the entire market to a squeaking standstill. I didn't even have to ask what I had done wrong. My shock reaction to their feigned shock reaction prompted a Russian man to explain that city maps were always a sensitive issue in border cities in the Belarus, or any former Soviet Union country for that matter. You require to be in central cities like Minsk or Moscow to receive a better response, let alone see maps of the city openly displayed for sale. I never saw a single map of the city of Brest within the city itself, at filling stations, in book shops, or souvenir shops to which they are part and parcel. This reality is however not advertised so that a lot of genuine tourists are bound to confront this experience sooner or later. Foreigners are not told before or when they have arrived that the act of them looking closely at a map will get them watched ever more closely by officials.

This pre-emptive strategy is also very evident in how powerful figures in society are busy as we speak creating the leaders every group of people need, rather than waiting for them to be born. The emergence of leaders in any group is in itself natural, connected to holism, or interplay of various factors performing their own predestined roles in the greater organism, crucial to its survival, that extends from the simplest of elements to the most complex. Those who become leaders are as such merely taking on roles assigned them by natural laws, whereas in societies where agendas exist these individuals are seen as crossing a line.

The pre-emptive strategy goes beyond mere leadership in society, as even the world of sport, music, film, knows its false stars.

Individuals who gain fame for one activity or another tend to become empowered, either due to the exposure they have to the public, or the means in monies that they suddenly attain. They become role models for some, while others will automatically side with their views. As such, these individuals have the potential to become a voice for many who agree with their style or ideas and identify with them. They may end up becoming the very channel by which anti government sentiment is expressed, or carried out.

It used to be the case even in old days that many music stars were simply selected, polished and marketed, but then at least there was enough room left for natural talent to manifest. Now, the point is to prevent anyone but the chosen few from succeeding. This thwarting is felt most among the talented who end up being unfairly targeted, especially because they are known to come standard supplied with abilities and capacities that are undesired for some people in power, or others with agendas. This repressive atmosphere has made it more difficult for real talent to even blossom, or survive, if they got that far, hence the reality there's a severe scarcity of them. This is a trend that has negatively impacted the international music scene, where the least worthy of attention are forced into our lives by way of the media, leading to a rise in the number of people retreating into sub-cultures where they can at least keep in touch with raw talent.

Anyone can sing, even rap, but it takes a special kind of talent to rouse people in manners only the most talented can, and this is precisely what people are realizing they miss in current pop stars, the point where the current experiment in phony leaders and stars is failing and being exposed.

Mentacide: Deliberate Destruction of the Mind

The covert warfare I became a victim of is that waged in the imperialistic realm against all who reside in countries considered the preserve of some countries. It partly falls under the category of economic and politically motivated attacks dealt with later, and partly under racially motivated attacks due to the adherence to bias typical of this system of apartheid.

This covert warfare has been going on for as long as modern day imperialism has lasted, a period where the methods have been refined; from the rudimentary where polio contaminated blankets were used as the covert weapon, to CONTELPRO, then the present where total annihilation or complete exclusion and marginalization is no longer the immediate objective. In such cases, the destruction of the mind of select victims has become the method of suppression of the concerned populations in readiness for the final solution.

In his article "Mentacide: The Ultimate Threat to the Black Race", the late Dr. Bobby Wright defines mentacide as "the deliberate and systematic destruction of a person's or group's mind" for the purpose of controlling that group, the end intention being extirpation.

Covert warfare to this end is limited to people of African descent wherever they may be. It crosses over territorial borders as need arises. As already intimated, the objective is to keep all considered the enemy docile, disempowered; importantly to keep them from realizing there is an actual undeclared war in progress, and what the aims and objectives of this war are.

The point of all covert warfare is to attack an enemy when their guard is lowered, when they are at their most vulnerable, making victory easier and less costly. It is meant to eliminate, or sometimes control this other's life, habitually involving the maiming or elimination of select people, as such maintaining a state of backwardness or powerlessness of the entire group that allows for easy control. Covert warfare conceals both the source of the aggression - who is behind such attacks, and the reason they are attacking people – a possible agenda or crime being covered up, so that the victims walk about not knowing if they are under attack, who is friend or foe, and when strange things happen to their lives they do not know why, nor do they realize why so many of their people are suffering and dying, believing things to be the way they have always been, or worse, believing this is just a bad turn in life that is bound to change.

There is increasing evidence in all parts of this planet where corporations have interests that suggest minorities and citizens in previously conquered countries qualify for exclusive consideration for this form of covert warfare, a duty that always falls on the government's intelligence agency in the countries that benefit from the corporations' activities. To this end, structures are in place whose sole aim is the identification and elimination of threats to the continued exploitation of resources in these lands. Such structures are distinct from those set up for control of local, especially indigenous or autochthonous populations by individual governments.

These structures carry out programs reminiscent of CONTELPRO. An entire outfit is created to spot and eliminate even very young people where they are considered potential threats to the status quo. Such attacks are of course not only limited to individual members, but can be launched against the entirety of communities or countries, especially residents of countries still controlled by, and considered the preserve of former colonizers.

All information we have been exposed to up till this day that reveals covert attacks involving chemicals, pathogens, or agents with the potential to lower the reproductive punch of a group, launched against Africans wherever they may be, had mentacide as the objective.

I will lead you through an anecdote that tells how I was attacked, that will hopefully reveal the existence of this international structure; international because it permeates national borders, and collaborates with similar structures in "third world" countries where leaders of governments are usually puppets who, trained to adopt any ways handed down from those to whom they have an inferiority complex, unknowingly adopt methods of keeping their opposition down that ultimately destroy indigenous culture.

I was a teenager when I left Africa and came to Europe to study at a university here. At the time, I already knew of ignorance, imperialism, colonialism, neo- colonialism, liberalism and neo-liberalism; one party politics, democracy, republicanism, protectionist policies, communism, etc. Though I was young, my convictions were firm. I was aware Africa was poor because of exploitation rooted in neo-colonial structures. I, like most African students that age, was convinced I had been exposed to all the knowledge necessary for a wholesome assessment of the issue, believing this knowledge contained the problem as well as the resolution.

That, however, was before I knew of the existence of this international structure whose sole purpose is to keep people in these parts of the planet in the dark by perpetually committing mentacide on them. As mentioned already, the methods of effecting the state are not restricted to attacks on individuals within the group, but extend to the health of the entirety of the group so that what comes out of them, be this ideas or offspring, ends up being second rate or degenerate.

I knew of the many puppets who shared a hand in Africa's fate, but only in the west did I get first hand experience of part of the process responsible for the creation of such monsters. This knowledge was gained either indirectly by plausible accounts of attempts at recruitment, then the covert terror unleashed against people who resisted. These were first hand accounts of methods of persecution that had previously been beyond my imagination, least of all the imaginations of most Africans.

It never happened to me, but I came face to face with Africans who were evidently being groomed for leadership roles in their countries of origin. These individuals would usually have friends in very high places who only showed up in rare instances, especially bailing them out of situations impossible to get out of without such connections. Noteworthy is the fact these Africans all shared one thing in common, which was that they were being trained to be beggar leaders, an attitude of most Africans in authority that works against the good of the whole. I also discovered the hard way that these individuals were also being trained in the tactics of covert warfare.

Despite everything, I am thankful I met these people, thankful that those who had refused recruitment also refused to be silenced and shared their experiences with me and a whole lot of other people. Of course, many were paying the ultimate price even as they related these experiences, but then I doubt whether I would have managed to survive what lay in wait for me had I not been introduced, as such prepared for the possibility that I would one day become one of the many Africans who are targeted because they are perceived as potential threats to the system.

I left school and decided to stay on in Europe to make some money that I could use to build a foundation when I returned. This decision would soon turn out to be the trigger of what followed, as well as the worst I have ever made in my life. Shortly after I got my very first job, I would enter a nightmare world that would last the better part of a decade, a period in which I struggled for my very sanity. I lost the respect of my family, struggled and won over physical states many considered permanent; and struggled to be published especially since the isolation had heightened within my person the need to be heard. When I finally got the exposure, I would find myself struggling to have the covert reality believed by indirect reference to it, for fear direct statements would get me certified as a mental case, which could potentially lay my chosen career to waste.

I realized I was a victim, as most people do, by the anomalous nature of the activities against me, which were designed to look normal when explained to the unsuspecting public. By testing things out, I was able to eventually know enough of the many avenues by which attacks were launched against me to gradually start the journey to complete self protection.

Despite a long period of awareness of the attacks, I only became sure of how long I had been a victim when the level of protection significantly reduced the symptoms that had been a more or less permanent reality as the cat and mouse game between me and my stalkers had progressed, situations when my body would heal as soon as I was in the clear, only to start all over again when my stalkers would step up their attacks to defeat the flimsy measures I put in place to protect myself. With the symptoms almost permanently removed, and my mind clear enough, I could look back to the time I first noticed the symptoms to know exactly and at what locale the attacks began.

I now know they started in mainland Europe, in Holland, following me through to every other European country I would later live in. They began with surreptitious entry into the privacy of my first apartment in my early twenties and then moved on to property that I would leave outside.

Initially, I only suspected such attacks were happening by the usual signs such people leave behind. Soon enough, accidentally, I happened upon concrete proof. I discovered the cylinder in the lock on my door broken, an act that was repeated as soon as I replaced the lock, repeated as many times as the lock was replaced, though nothing was ever stolen from my house.

The cars I owned were all tampered with, so that most of the time I would walk into the car, looking well, but would walk out feeling dizzy and looking dishevelled. At first, I believed it was the atmosphere within the vehicle, but when the symptoms remained after almost religious dedication to cleaning. After going through different vehicles but experiencing the same symptoms, I concluded it was just an allergy. This was until I observed other people's straight features turn as bloated as mine after they had been in any one of my vehicles long enough, whereas the phenomenon was not repeated when I traveled in their vehicles. Only then did it became plain it was not an allergy, a gas leak that all my vehicles had in common, but that there was more to the story than met the eye.

I have experienced sharp, burning sensations in my fingers, that would culminate in pain in my joints after handling a bike I left parked outside while I attended to some business, have had a numb behind after sitting on a motorcycle, suffering subsequently from a weak, painful back for a period after that.

I have been gassed and almost taken out while in my own house, surviving only by strength, luck, and a stubbornness that saw me wearing gas masks in my own home. I discovered that the gas attacks would almost always start when I was asleep, when I would suddenly wake actually tasting and sensing the toxic substances in the atmosphere around, gasping for air, eyes teary. I discovered that the attacks would be timed with all activities that reduced sensitivity to attacks, for example beer drinking when the mind can easily mistake the effects. I would always wake up in a state after a bout of drinking at home, whereas when I drank and subsequently spent the night outside the hangover would not be as toxic, even when the pre-drinking and post-drinking routine was the same.

To ascertain this, I tried wearing a gas mask in my house while drinking; only removing the mask to take a swig at my beer, then in a hotel room nobody would have expected me to go to, making sure I drank as much as I usually do. I became sure of what was happening when I didn't wake up with the same toxic taste in my mouth on all occasions I tried an alternative method or location.

I have had activities within the four walls of my own private space told me by total strangers while out and about. Here, I am not referring to activities that sensory organs can pick up, for example smells, sounds, etc. I ascertained this by various methods of elimination, as it became essential for me to find out whether my neighbors were reacting to me the way they were because I was overly offensive.

I had a neighbor who would react in a given manner whenever I embarked on certain activities, a time I almost came to believe preparation or contemplation of some activities could be picked up by the senses before the actual event. Closer scrutiny, and a lot of feigning on my part to test this out, soon revealed the reaction could not always be connected to sensory perceptions, nor was it based on predictions. This neighbor made the same scrambling noises no matter what time it was, whenever I started exercising, started cooking, or started eating.

He could remain silent the entire day, only making sounds when he would occasionally go out of his room to the toilet, take a walk, go to the kitchen, etc., only to return to his room, be silent, then make the same series of sounds as soon as I engaged in specific activities, some that could hardly be picked up by the senses; such as typing on my laptop, reading a book under my breath (a practice I have kept since my school days that I find refreshing to the senses). He would make the same scrambling noises when I turned on or started using a small gadget (a torch, a mobile phone, a pocket radio, apart from the larger appliances, e.g. TV, Stereo).

I soon took it for granted that I was being monitored 24/7. This became increasingly obvious when unjustified intrusions into my personal life became part and parcel of my daily experience on the streets, as total strangers took every opportunity to reveal what I had sent in my email, what I had done in my room the previous night, who I called and what we talked about, even discussing the content of an article I had just sent to a publisher even though it was yet to be published, etc. They obviously had my phone tapped, were always tuned into my internet activity, but for the rest I guessed they were using microphones, heat sensor, infrared or magnetic imaging equipment to observe me through the walls.

There is no reason why I deserved such close monitoring. I was not involved in any activity that could pose a danger as high as would require such close scrutiny, an activity illegal in itself. I could not possibly have been the worst person in the city, if anyone who lives in such locations knows the various kinds of personalities who are its denizens, who do not attract such surveillance and harassment as a result of their idiosyncratic natures. One thing I am sure of was the repressive intention, as seen in the constant attempts to tell me they knew what I was doing at every turn, which would turn into real threats of violence especially when they would find me walking the streets all recovered and shining, realizing I was successfully fending off attacks.

The experience in my own flat was not the worst yet, since by having my own house there were ways I could shut the stalking out. After a short spell in prison for a civil offense I should not have been punished for under normal circumstances, I became homeless after running out of a homeless shelter where attacks became too dangerous to risk being exposed to. I made several accommodation applications, and finally, a charity organization came to my rescue. It was a single room in a run down but well furnished flat where 8 other males rented rooms.

I accepted the offer and made payment arrangements, only to discover that I had been set up. Upon entry into the house, I experienced hounding by some of the tenants from the get go, for no good reason whatsoever, often with threats of violence that I knew were pre-planned, had nothing to do with whatever was happening in the flat, and if they had then the effect was deliberately induced in order for them to react to it in the manner they did.

Everything that happened on these premises was a repeat of what had gone on in other locations, with the major difference of intensity and the fact the tenants themselves made it plain they were harassing me. Fortunately for me at this time, I had already done sufficient research on the subject and was enlightened enough to know what I was now confronted with. I knew for example that I was being baited. The people setting me up knew I lacked fear. They knew of especially my physical prowess, this having been made perfectly clear when I had to hold my own in prison. Sizing the new gang of stalkers, I realized they were nowhere near what I could easily handle. The people who had put them up to the activities were obviously also aware of this fact, but were waiting for the moment I would lose it and lash out.

The overt and constant harassment was meant to elicit a reaction. I would however be considered guilty even though I had not done anything wrong, according to false accounts many "witnesses" would give. What would be waiting around the corner was re-arrest by the very people who had put me in the very position, and the torture I had already experienced under the exclusion of a jailing system where space has been created for such activities to be carried out unnoticed.

I had survived illegal arrest due to the fact I had already impacted the literary scene on a worldwide scale, and the authorities were forced to release me after some public outrage at my illegal arrest. My pursuers were now trying to force me into committing a real crime in order to get me back where I could be controlled much more effectively Instead of just one neighbor reacting to whatever I did, I had the person who lived below, and two next to me reacting in predictable manners. My new neighbors also had the potential to see right through my walls, also reacting predictably to activities within my four walls that were as exact as the other cases, but then they didn't make any secret of it. I had heard statements thrown at me by strangers on the streets, but never had these strangers thrown these statements into my face, at pains to provoke a response, as these new neighbors did.

There was also the added reality that the very air I breathed would change drastically every time I for example started typing on my laptop, started doing some exercises, or started eating. What's worse is these new neighbors had no qualms in informing me these attacks were indeed poisons.

They would also respond loudly to any sound I made, any statement made under my breath. In this new house, I could not even be alone in my mind.

It was impossible to hear vocal sounds through the walls in this house, other than footsteps or objects dropped. I would for example only know my neighbor had his television on or was engaged in a phone conversation when I walked past his door, not when I was in my room. As such, according to the direct responses I got whenever I would talk to myself, even in a low voice, whenever my phone rang and I answered, the sudden rush of footsteps every time I whispered to myself or started typing, the other occupants could obviously hear a pin drop in my room.

Visitors to my house were harassed, so that they thought twice before coming to see me. Those that spent the night would get followed wherever they went in the house, complaining about the man who seemed to have nothing to do but just stand there, observing them. This was the resident "crack head" who was not too discrete about the issue to anyone. He would openly brag about his bravery in confronting me, and the unlikelihood I would do anything about what was happening to me because I was a coward.

A friend or family member's approach would always be anticipated, so that the weirdest displays would ensue as soon as he/she would be approaching the property. Violence would erupt between people who lived in the house, knives would be brandished and carried around threateningly; voices would be raised for the duration. Sound systems would have the volume set to levels intolerable even to the people doing this. Individuals would deliberately let their food burn, as such filling the house with smells and smoke, the noise from the smoke alarms becoming intolerable.

These activities reached a crescendo when the visitor had actually arrived. Then, I would get people who had never before knocked on my door entering my room, voices raised, at times with knives on the display.

They made me aware they were constantly watching me, but how well remained unknown to me until one particular incident. There was this man who spent the least days in the flat because he was evicted by the landlord for rowdy conduct. I meditate a lot, and follow this through with slow physical exercises replicating karate moves. This is good for balance as well as the mind. I was busy doing this exercise one day in the summer, with curtains drawn, when I heard coughing and splattering outside my window. I looked out from the first floor, onto the backyard below and saw this man whose reaction made me realize at once the splattering had been aimed at attracting my attention. There he stood, simulating the motions I had just been going through, right down to the last point, though he could hardly keep his balance as well as I could.

These weird displays in front of my window continued for a while, and stopped when tenants not involved with the stalking informed the landlord, who soon after evicted the man.

I could not personally have gone to the extent of reporting the activity to my landlord. I have long since stopped involving people in this issue, even though I realize my landlord would get attacked anyway for the simple fact he had allowed me to stay for as long as he did. The reason I have stopped involving people directly, preferring for the indirect method is because I discovered that when people really believed my accounts, they would soon after report unusual events with their own lives. Sometimes, I didn't even need to explain, as the people who had been harassing me had usually become so confident they left signs that others could easily pick up, a good example being the case of the man above. In one other instance, long before the horror in the flat above, a friend accidentally discovered my place was being broken into.

I was moving a previous tenant's furniture out of my flat one day when a friend came visiting. As I was leaving, with my hands full, I requested that he get the keys from my pocket and lock the door for me. He did this, but soon discovered that the key kept turning indefinitely in the lock. He informed me of this, after which I revealed this had happened to a few other locks that I had replaced for the reason. My local locksmith had only shrugged when asked why my locks were breaking down like this, but from my friend, I learnt that this only happened when the cylinder was broken, which is what happens when certain locks are picked. He asked whether I had been robbed in the past, to which I gave the honest answer: nothing had ever been removed from my home since I moved in.

Before that time, I had been engaged in a steady relationship with a German lady, and had rented the flat out for a limited period to save money. When I returned after the rent period had elapsed, I changed the lock the tenant had placed in the door to prevent entry by anyone who had a copy of the key, but not before checking and ascertaining the lock I was removing had not had its cylinder broken. A week after this, the cylinder of the new lock had been broken. Whoever had been making covert entries into the premises had not been interested in the other tenant, the particular property, but me.

I do not know whether my friend told others about this event, but I do know something happened because after this he became a victim of repeated break-ins himself, the results that I witnessed personally, losing most of his valuables as a result. He informed the police who didn't do anything, and finally just left the country.

Fortunately for him, he had the wherewithal in a relative who listened and believed, then gave the financial aid, and also the presence of mind to make the proper move, whereas in my case, for the duration this has been going on, I have seldom had the wherewithal, and when I have, have lacked the presence of mind to save myself by relocation. The few cases where I came close to saving myself have seen reactions from some unknown source in society that stopped me in my tracks. This has to date included sudden arrest, release from prison in the middle of the night followed by intense attacks in a Christian hostel, or the untraceable removal of funds from my own bank account.

I was arrested right after I had completed my first book, just when I sent the manuscript to a publishing house. In jail, I was confronted head on with the psychopathic racial personality that Dr. Wright describes in his article named before. While I languished behind bars, I watched a television program in which an emerging African author's new work was presented, a novel remarkably similar to the one on the manuscript I had sent for publication consideration, right down to the four parts that mine had consisted of; including the rooting in Afro- centricity or the African worldview. This was far from mere coincidence since it is highly unlikely that two African writers could at the same time write prose pieces around the same issue, arranged identically.

The author's point of view was heard in the interview, and it became obvious as he spoke that he wasn't in the least articulate; not the mental apparatus you would expect any intellectual work to come from.

I was released six months later, after which I was forced to rewrite the entire book from scratch, the copy manuscripts having gone missing while I languished in jail.

All of this notwithstanding, I started writing articles again, but soon experienced harassment as soon as the first got published, that came in the form of intimidating statements from strangers on the streets, warning me to stop writing; explicitly reminding me what had happened in prison; making me aware this would be repeated if I did not comply.
I also noticed that when a publisher had a website where the article was also published, it would get hacked so that it became unavailable for some time. To date, this has happened so often it cannot be coincidence. One website that consistently published my articles was attacked and brought down, and has literally never been allowed back up again.

Looking back, I realize this culmination was inevitable, as I vaguely became aware even at the time I undertook activities that traditionally attract such wrath. This last statement may imply I knew all along why I was targeted, but dared the local bully anyway, but then there existed in my mind doubt as to whether such activity could indeed attract such wrath, despite a lot of indicators.

I was naïve, believing like many do that all freedoms were granted every individual in western countries. I thought you could do whatever you want in the west, as long as you didn't impinge on another's rights. The west was after all the home of the free, compared to my country of origin where you could get arrested for saying the wrong thing about a local politician. I am certain now that this notion is a myth, though at the time it was a vague suspicion. I know now the promotion of this false idea constitutes the trap the unwary world is bound to walk into sooner or later.

I, like most who come to the west to study, was not aware extra-curricula education of a certain kind that involved gaining knowledge for the sake of it was frowned upon. There are books in western libraries that are not intended for the general public. There is information displayed for the general public that is not meant for especially African people to be exposed to. This includes books that tell of the real history of the race, the history of racial relationships, books with the potential to change how a person thinks about identity and race, permanently.

Some of the material I read was bought from local book stores, but the vast majority was borrowed from libraries, most of it either so esoteric or rare it had to be ordered from other sources. If someone got interested in what I was spending sleepless nights reading, they could easily get the list from the library I frequented, or the bookstore. In fact, looking back, I know someone somewhere did just this, and they didn't like what they were seeing. I got a few indicators of this at the time. I remember hearing a few comments by total strangers that questioned my choice of books, though, unfortunately, I didn't make much of this.

Another side to this is the reality I was actually getting a lot of breaks in my adopted, European country, sometimes even more so than locals. There were even complaints made to this effect. I didn't realize then that there was a price I needed to pay for the breaks. I could not have believed whatever magnanimous figure(s) giving me the breaks would have simultaneously wished to restrict me in such a manner, never thought any human being could harbor thoughts of this kind. This truth became apparent gradually, the hard way.

I sometimes blame myself for walking into this trap. This is because, prior to my making the realization, prior to me positively identifying instances of such attacks, a few people had warned me of the possibility of such an eventuality, people who happened to be both white and African, young, middle aged, and old.

Three cases are etched in my memory, two involving white men, young and old, and one involving an African intellectual who'd previously been a successful businessman in a different European country from the one in which we met.

In the first case, I was out with a group of African friends when this grey, gaunt white man approached us. He started speaking to the group, but then eventually shifted his attention to me in a manner indicating I had been what had attracted his attention in the first place. Then, looking me sternly in the eye, he directed the words "they'll never let you" at me. At this point, my friends stopped wondering whether the man was insane, and started making distance, but he had somehow managed to raise my curiosity to the point I could not follow suit. As the rest shuffled out of reach, leaving me standing there with a strange old white man holding my hand, talking even stranger things, I asked what he meant. He repeated the statement, at which point I lost patience and condescendingly asked who "they" were, and why they would select me, and not that, or that man. Without taking his eyes off me, the old man shook his head, tears suddenly welling in his eyes, finally, and surprisingly lucidly explained what he meant. According to this man, I fit the profile of one who would inevitably get in trouble for doing something that's not allowed for kind in this time.

I have since left that European country, but would later experience versions of this same event in a number of locations. Another case involved a white national of a country different from the first. Though this time he didn't include the historical element, he spoke from experience. He didn't address me, but made sure I knew the message was intended for me from across the pub table. Unlike the previous case, this man made it plain, to his friend, how it was done.

"They destroy their minds" were the words that came from the white man's mouth, who suddenly and strangely relapsed into an emotional state, tears falling freely.

These words and the methods would later be told to me in detail by a harassed African I befriended a few years later, again in a different country. He was a formerly successful businessman who happened to have done extensive studies of ancient African history, especially the spirituality of these ancients that he would bring alive in a manner nobody had ever done before. This man was illegally in the country, fleeing from what he said was systematic persecution in another part of Europe where he had run a successful business. He divulged his business methods, claiming the success to be well within reach of anybody who cared to listen and learn. He was on the run, but had discovered that as long as he remained within the frontiers of Europe, or countries that remained colonies of the same lands, he was within reach of these people.

I have since heard this same story repeated by all manner of nationals, and, in the case of Africans, the incidences have almost always involved business success and subsequent systematic persecution by a strata of the population so large and equipped, yet invisible and largely unknown to general society, it is beyond most people's imaginations. Most of us, including me before this happened, believe this place to be a concrete jungle where much is possible. We believe every man we meet on the streets is a stranger who has his own business, whereas the reality is that there is an agenda in place to which a significant percentage of the population are privy, who we meet on a daily basis, some of whom become our spouses and friends, even bear children with us, as long as this is in line with the success of this agenda.

Though similar stories have come from Africans, Diaspora Africans, White Europeans, even an account by a Chinese national who was sent fleeing under such attacks, from America where he had been naturalized, through Europe till he made it back to his country of origin; there is a peculiar manner that continental Africans and Diaspora Africans are attacked, a violence of such intensity and savagery unlike the other cases, that points to the existence of a program the aims of which Dr. Bobby Wright describes in his article.

What is frightening is the reality the people behind this have been doing it for as long as Africans have been a conquered folk, and by now have enough knowledge to tell off one African from another, enough knowledge to know lineages and blood, so that, in this hemisphere, with the pre-emptive strategy gone awry, some of us will inevitably end up targets, no matter what we do, if by this we can be prevented from reaching the verge where the next step cannot be prevented without overt spilling of blood.

Relational and Other Problems

Covert warfare that falls under this heading is that which arises out of personal disputes culminating in revenge, vengeance, punishment, or retribution campaigns that manifest as perpetual harassment or intent to do harm. The disputes are usually between family members or families, neighbors, scorned spouses, etc.

Such campaigns can be carried out by the party involved themselves, or a criminal, or group of criminals they hire to do the job for them. These campaigns are limited in scope as the means of a single individual to maintain sustained attacks over a prolonged period is limited. Where a gang of people is hired for the purpose, the financial resources and capacity to control activities of those hired by one individual limits the intensity or length such activities can be carried out. It also limits more especially the kinds of know-how and technologies that can be applied for the purpose, as this will depend on the exposure of the individual or the gang he/she chooses at random to such knowledge.

Under this heading also fall cases of celebrity stalking, which are situations where normal adulation, hero worship, adoration or admiration of an individual celebrity has gone wrong and crossed over into an obsession where the celebrity is actually stalked.

As mentioned already, these activities are one off occurrences that start and end when the objective has been achieved, or when the wherewithal has run out. This could be when the gang hired for the purpose can no longer be properly controlled, trusted or paid, or when the target has been driven mad, led to their demise or immigration from the city or country. What should be noted here is such crimes seldom follow the victim when they have moved out of a city, whereas in cases where higher authority is involved the TI can not stop the prosecution even when he/she moves to a different country. This is mostly true in cases where officials in the country chosen for relocation are allied on the cause.

In cases where a businessperson is targeting their former employee, the same conditions apply. Furthermore, unlike the variant of the crime where citizens are targeted at random, at times for no good reason whatsoever, the public accepts the existence of attacks of this nature, many of which have come to our attention through the media, especially when the perpetrators have been caught and brought to justice.

Xenophobic and Racial

Under this umbrella fall cases where groups in society target minorities, including recent immigrants, on racial grounds. These attacks can take on a much more aggressive and sinister nature than the former since significant segments of society can be rallied for the cause, as such providing for a wide base that can be relied upon for sustained attacks and funding. Better methods and technologies are available for the same reasons. Such attacks sometimes stray into the realm of the politically motivated, especially cases where the stalkers are known to be carrying out the government's dirty work for them, which in many instances has been exposed as being the case with a lot of right wing organizations in many countries, more especially the KKK.

Victims of such attacks include the autochthonous who are friendly to foreigners, have relationships with foreigners, homosexuals, those with mental and physical deformities, etc.

Political and Economic

Whistleblowers and activists are the most known instances of people who engender such attacks, and the offenders are corporations, or governments. The two merge in interest when governments act as instruments of corporate policy, so that the target is considered a risk by both, for the same reasons.

These cases are not restricted to regions, so that moving does not stop the problem. As already stated, some countries cooperate on a lot of issues, or certain structures are international, so that the terror is bound to continue as long as the TI chooses the wrong country to run to. In cases where corporations are acting alone, they have enough resources to make the harassment they mete out as formidable and permanent as government harassment.

Chapter 5

Dispelling Doubt

In This Chapter
- Clearing the Fog Of Doubt
- Weighing Security System Vulnerabilities
- Personalized Security Systems
- Mobile Home: the Last Resort

In his book "Terrorist Stalking in America", David Lawson states: *"Some countries kill dissidents and in others they are jailed. In the united states, someone who is threatening to corporations or industries, like a whistle blower or activist, is likely to become the target of an extremist group."* David Lawson spent a lot of time monitoring the activities of these extremist groups, and gained a lot of inside knowledge on their modus operandi.

Lawson's book is useful as it will familiarize the reader with the inner workings of such groups, and the connections they have with government, law enforcement, and other social institutions, especially the degree of infiltration, so that they, rather than the conscientious, are running the show.

I find that his statement distinguishing methods of elimination between countries is a hastily arrived at conclusion that verges on an assumption. The reality is that, because of the real danger of waking and invoking the wrath of the sleeping masses, all governments avoid overt elimination of threats. They use groups similar in nature to those that exist in the west, set up for the purpose, usually linked to their intelligence agencies, that do not necessarily resemble extremist groups of the kind known to exist in America or other western countries.

This is possible for the universally known reality it does not take extremists to create such groups, as society always has an abundance of individuals capable of carrying out the dirty work of people in power. In fact, we can speak of the existence of all methods in almost all parts of the world. It is a well known fact that activists are still thrown in jail in America or Europe, are disgraced publicly, and in some instances bumped off in so called accidents, suicides, or that they meet their demise at the hands of some activist or deranged person, as well as become targets of extremist groups. Each method of elimination is suited to the circumstances, the overt method usually only becoming useful when it is too late to employ slow-kill methods, when all else has failed.

On top of that, there are connections between governments that the average citizen is not aware of, whereby certain governments have in the past received support of one kind or another that commits them to carrying out activities requested by the other. It is then in the best interest of one government to give its knowledge on methods of threat elimination to the other, ensuring that its interests are taken care of by people trusted to do a good job of it. This means that, as citizens, we will be confronted with the same system wherever we go. Good news is that the same methods of coping with attacks in the western sphere can also be used successfully in countries outside of it.

Depending on what you are doing, attacks may start off covertly, without warning, so that you will only discover along the way that you are a victim, usually when it is too late and the damage has been done. Other times there are warnings given. These may be threats to one's life or property that are connected to recent activity that is felt as threatening by certain segments of society. There may be times when attacks start off with overt damage to property, repeated forced entry and the like.

It is not always a problem to tell you are under attack, and know who is attacking, when you already know the kind of activities you are engaged in could prompt reactions of this nature from those in power. It is also easy to know you could potentially become a target of covert attacks when there are warnings given, threats on your life, especially when you are in the know that such threats are not bluffs. Identifying the first attacks then becomes easy, and surviving them depends on how much knowledge the targeted individual has at their disposal for self defense.

The vast majority of people are attacked for reasons that have little if nothing to do with what they are currently doing, those when the elimination is pre-emptive. Here, depending on the method of incapacitation employed, the target may either only discover they have been under attack when they are already isolated from society, or when they observe symptoms of disease that are the result of the more lethal kind of attacks. Sometimes they never even know they have been under attack, the last thing they are aware of being the stroke, heart attack, or a brain tumor that suddenly or progressively kills them.

Because these attacks are covert, they are in most cases designed to physically affect the mind of the victim so that not only his potential to pose a threat is minimized, but also his capacity to make sense of the situation, to tell one thing from another, which may unfortunately also include doubt in the individual's mind of whether they are really under attack. The community to which the individual belongs will usually harbor no such doubts, leaving the target alone in the matter.

As mentioned already in this book, it is possible, indeed necessary considering the present state of world affairs, to take on board the kind of measures and precautions advised in this book even when you are sure you are not a victim of covert warfare. It is always a good idea to be prevention oriented, but for those who currently suspect they are under covert attack, it is crucial that you ascertain this state, especially that you know what kind of attack you are under as this will help in devising targeted measures that will simplify the process of coping with the attacks, saving you money, energy and time.

Though not absolutely necessary, knowing why you became a victim helps since attacks are usually tailored to the level of threat. Incapacitation campaigns against a potential threat in a person who has not done anything are seldom lethal, but involve the defiling of that particular individual's mind, so that the threat potential is diminished, while those against figures who are known publicly follows different routes altogether. In some cases, attacks will only cease with the demise of the target, while in others they will cease as soon as there are enough signs pointing to a permanent change in lifestyle. Some are meant to force people to behave in certain ways, while others are designed to kill.

You need to take in all the activities you were involved in right before the attacks began, and using the knowledge gained about why people become targets, single out the activities or acquaintances that caused such attacks. You might discover that severing some relationships might stop the attacks, while in other cases it may not. The point here is the range of suspect activities determines the type of attack, sometimes giving you options that may stop the attacks.

Clearing the Fog of Doubt

Test everything out so that you are sure the effect you have noticed is not induced by factors unrelated to covert warfare, and if so then conduct further tests to determine what is being used against you. For example, if you are experiencing unusual discomforts in your own home, find out as soon as possible whether this is restricted to your home; as soon as possible because symptoms can become permanent after prolonged exposure to harmful substances. Spend some time in another location and see if there is noticeable change. If you are being harassed by people you meet on the streets, try to walk through the same streets with another person and see whether the same happens.

There is a kind of behavior a target will identify in people who harass them, one they will identify even when they are with other people and no harassment occurs. If you do recognize stalkers though no harassment occurs when in the company of another, then you have the proof you need it does not have anything to do with any fault of yours.

Carefully formulated thoughts on how the situation came about will be useful as they will not only provide a lasting account of the process that led to such a culmination, but ensure the verity of present perceptions as this can only be the inevitable result. Realizations once reached should be recorded as the mind may become unreliable for such rationalizations once the attacks proceed beyond a given intensity. Such accounts, while definitely useful for the victim, can also be used to introduce others to issues and difficulties involved in identifying causes, through discovery that results by personally going through elimination of factors that create uncertainty.

One such factor is disease, mental or physical, a symptom that most victims of attack share in common as a direct result of such attacks, but which could also be the cause for the perceptions.

Medical tests are a must for a person in this situation, as only the results from such will provide information required to know for sure whether the symptoms are a result of disease or not. However, for various reasons, victims of covert warfare may feel reluctant to rely on results of such tests. One of these would be knowledge effects from such attacks can be misinterpreted, especially when there is damage to the immune system or there is a low t-cell count. A result based on such calculations could end a victim of covert warfare on a cure that may add to the problem, side effects and all, because it does not address the actual cause.

Many may also have suspicions about medical institutions, especially in cases where the stalking has come from too many segments of society, enough to create the lasting impression that almost every social institution is infiltrated. If the mind is still intact, then the last place such an individual would like to be is a clinic or hospital, where the chance exists the people handling the case, whatever their nationality, race or religion, could be in on the conspiracy.

Developing a deeper understanding of disease and how it manifests, whether mental or physical, and staying in touch with your personal experience of the diseases you suffered before, is a good way of avoiding the possibility of wrongly diagnosing a state. For example, if you have suffered from fever before, then you will identify the difference between an actual fever caused by a certain pathogen, and another induced by your living environment, not only through the symptoms at varying levels of infection, but by the usual course the disease follows. Unlike naturally caused symptoms of fever, an artificially induced fever may be restricted to certain locations, articles of clothing, etc. This information can also be used to dispel chronic conditions from affecting conclusions you reach about the source of the symptoms.

Exposing yourself to as much information on conditions that resemble yours, but also becoming very health conscious in your life helps a lot.

Depending on whether you know what you are being attacked with or not, there are medications you can take, and processes you can undergo to ameliorate the effects, even rid the system of toxicants and mend damaged tissue. Physical exercise, vitamin and mineral supplements are a must for people under attack. How you should exercise and what supplements to take is dealt with in detail in "chapter 11".

I will lead by example here, and hopefully not only provide an account that provides food for thought, but dispel in the reader's mind any lingering thoughts of the possibility I have diagnosed my situation wrongly, if I have not done so already, whether there isn't another reason for what I experienced.

It is important to remember before you proceed that those who commit such crimes rely on the creation of doubt within the mind of their victim, and the populace at large to succeed. They require the target to not only see self in the wrong light, but to be seen by the population at large as mentally unstable, corrupt, suffering from delusions… whatever suits the purpose. If their health starts to ail and they perish, then this should be seen as resulting from natural causes.

I have noticed with dismay that the general public's degenerate understanding of symptom and disease is a point these criminals exploit to the fullest, especially in African communities. This has been more so with the advent of HIV/AIDS, the "all symptom" disease that usually steps in to take credit for whatever is happening to an individual. I clearly remember growing up at a time when there was a better understanding and attitude towards disease, that in large part was due to acceptance disease was part of life, unlike today when stigma can be attached to being sick. People may not have known as many diseases as they do today, nor could they tell every disease by the symptom, but the general attitude towards disease was so healthy it could not have been abused in the manner it is now. The present attitude actually provides the cloak by which a lot of people are felled while we watch, since we will associate any unhealthy condition we see with one singular disease, that everybody suspects is making surreptitious rounds in their community.

The fault lies in the manner authority launched their awareness and prevention campaigns through the media. The first leg was the abuse of the people's sensibilities, turning this in on itself so that they started prosecuting the sick, witch hunting and suspecting each other and self, only to become ashamed and frightened to face consequences of actual infection at a time when they least needed it. This went on to the point everything that could be wrong with a person was considered to emanate from this singular source. Then, symptoms of disease that would otherwise not fit by the profile of any known disease, and would as such raise eyebrows and provoke questions and investigations, were brushed off as HIV/AIDS.

This state of affairs would have been impossible in the past. I remember in my younger days when we would ask adults questions, and get proper responses about diseases: how to detect symptoms, and prevent infection, a time when some of us became very good at determining what the other could be suffering from depending on the symptoms. Nowadays, our youth have no such discerning powers. Everything has been narrowed down to the disease in vogue in their minds.

People under psychological or physical attack usually exhibit symptoms of real disease, and would be much better helped if they didn't have society reacting to them as if they are the problem. This just adds to the stress and isolation. Nobody in the target community wins since the attacks, though sometimes aimed at individuals, are actually meant to keep the whole group down.

By so saying, I am not encouraging unsafe sex, merely pointing out the need for individuals within this situation to take every opportunity to raise their level of awareness on disease, as that within the group at large, especially concerning attitudes towards people suspected of suffering from disease, as only this will prevent target communities themselves indirectly aiding attacks on them. A different attitude towards disease, but especially an in depth knowledge of especially covert warfare, and what such attacks can do to people, could help greatly in minimizing the turmoil victims of covert attacks have to go through, while at the same time aiding in closing avenues of attack.

I have been sick before in my life; have survived malaria, have had fevers, and all manner of diseases, most of this happening when I was much younger, so I pretty much know what it feels like to be sick. What I started feeling when the attacks started was nowhere near what I had felt when one pathogen or other had invaded my body. It was realistically similar to what is commonly felt when, for example, people experiment with various drugs, or when you turn a fire on in a badly ventilated room.

Body fluid samples, chest scans and vital organ tests still indicated I was healthy, even at times when the symptoms from the attacks were at a zenith. I could as such still take as much alcohol as I did before the attacks began, and wake up feeling well, and could still do heavy exercises that are beyond the average person's capacities, for prolonged periods, without suffering from symptoms the day after.

At this time, before I ditched the bad habit of beer drinking that actually aids attacks, and learnt how to protect myself from most attacks, I suffered from blurred vision, had painful joints, this coinciding with days when I would feel as though I was sleeping in a room pumped full of toxins, waking up feeling a burning sensation at the back of my neck. I have noticed strait white lines along my nails, all of these strong indicators of heavy metal poisoning, rather than some disease.

Thankfully, I no longer have any recurring conditions that could complicate the issue, though I had malaria before I became a teenager, and know the disease can never completely be cured. I know how a malaria attack feels, and experienced a number of recurrences when I was much younger, that stopped somewhere in my early adulthood, never to be repeated again.

I have never had a venereal disease, have not had the common cold for a while, and the last time I had it, which from this date in 2006 would be two years ago, it was not severe enough to even register. These are facts people who see me on a daily basis can testify to. It is very easy to know by the sniffing and blowing that the person going by has a cold, and easier still to identify the person if he is perpetually sick in the same manner, therefore very easy to tell cases of suppressed immunity from symptoms, rather than looks. I hope and pray, as is normal for everybody, that I stay as healthy as I have been so far; even though the debilitations on my body from the attacks I endured when I didn't know how to protect myself may have taken that much more off the top of my health and life span. I remain confident they have not.

When I first became convinced I was being stalked by the number of people who openly revealed personal, private things to me, when I isolated my house as the point where most of the physical attacks were occurring, I became a denizen in the doctor's waiting room in the hope the notion I was getting tested would deter the attacks. At the time, I was also certain the tests would reveal what I was being attacked with.

Several blood and other sample tests later, my doctor became convinced I was a hypochondriac, and suggested therapy. This came as a major blow to me because I had hoped any positive result would vindicate me and prove my sanity to those I had told of the occurrences. Such results ruled out the kind of poisoning I thought I was a victim of. But then by proving my blood was not poisoned, that I didn't have the auto-brewery syndrome I suspected when a few random police tests showed alcohol levels above the legal limit, even though I had not touched alcohol or any other similar substance for weeks, I knew there was something wrong with the results. I harbored deep suspicion of medical institutions for a period after that, the need to know the truth so pressing I even went to the extent of using a friends identity papers for tests, which produced the same results. In my mind the doubt remained as I felt I was watched and followed even when I went to the hospital with a different identity. In fact, those who would usually openly tell me secrets about my life also reacted angrily to this attempt at covert tests, fostering this last belief.

The single most destructive aspect of being a victim of covert warfare is the lack of certainty that is usually a direct result of such attacks, but more importantly the fact society has a vested interest in keeping the problem hushed so that people cannot come out openly and state they are victims. It is the aim of those who wage such warfare to induce in the victim, as well as the society at large, a state of mind that conceals the source of such activities. It becomes necessary therefore to maintain as clear a mental state as is possible, in this case by applying a system of elimination to every situation you are confronted with, as such dispelling much of the doubt that may lead into an actual, delusional state.

Weighing Security System Vulnerabilities

Victims of gaslighting experience subtle changes to their environment, tampering of their personal property, which can also include destructive alterations to professional work. This means the harassers are regularly entering the target's space, and could be tampering with much more than inanimate, non-food objects in the house. In fact, there is no reason why they would limit their activities to, for example, moving furniture around and not tamper with what the victim consumes. This becomes more evident in light of lethal intentions of some attacks. If they can use energy beams to eventually kill the target, then they might as well poison his/her food supply to achieve the same, given the chance.

Though the best advice out there encourages victims to live with other people, to avoid being isolated, the fact of the matter is the property of a mature male or female is always easy to identify, even when he/she lives with a family, even when they are all adults like the target. Some degree of study will always reveal what a particular individual's personal preferences are, especially the products he/she prefers to consume or use, which cannot always be identical to another, unless by design.

There will always come that moment when the home is vacated, when the perpetrators can easily walk in and pick out the property they know belongs to the target, to tamper with for desired results. This is why it is important that as soon as a targeted individual discovers they are under covert attack they personally close as many avenues of attack as they can, and the best place to start is with security. It makes no sense relying on the knowledge having people around by itself permanently removes the threat, which could lead to the dangerous lowering of the guard.

Noteworthy is the fact that there are those methods of installing security that only work when the TI lives alone. I will give examples of how they can be adapted to different situations, but I doubt these will suffice to cover all the scenarios out there that a TI may be confronted with. TI's will need to look at personal circumstances to see how they can adapt such measures to other situations.

Good security systems are usually very expensive, and understandably beyond the means of a person under covert attack. This is because when successful, such attacks ensure the victim doesn't have much access to a descent means of earning a living. It is however possible to install security that is cheap and simple in ways that make it much more secure. This involves the combining of security systems, or, in the extreme case, the personalization of a system.

Combining and personalization of security systems involves replacing or augmentation of parts with others that do not come standard supplied with a device, as such changing how the system works or how and for what it is applied, or placing components or personalized objects on the device that make a mark identifiable to one, and non-alterable by another without leaving signs of tampering. Basically, it involves playing around with simple systems in order to either make the result difficult to bypass because it is unknown, overcoming inherent vulnerabilities where they exist, or preventing tampering of the security device, for example the picking of a padlock

There is very little awareness out there that expensive equipment isn't all it's hyped out to be. Most security systems being pandered as "cutting edge" have vulnerabilities that make their installation superfluous. What's worse is some systems provide as such a false sense of security.

One major flaw with high security systems is the fact they are all mass produced, and come in models. Attacking groups already have extensive knowledge of some models, while the unknown are usually easily bypassed on the basis of knowledge already gained from other, sometimes cheaper systems and devices. This is because the technology used in the production of most security systems is similar, and in most instances the same components are used, albeit altered in model name, shape and appearance.

As a result of being a target, I did a lot of research on spy shop products for gadgets I could use to defend myself against covert attacks. I discovered the hard way, after spending fortunes on fancy, expensive gadgets, that there are a lot of devices that can only be used for specific purposes, others that may work well for common thieves but are no match for thugs connected to the intelligence services, with access to advanced equipment and knowledge. Some of these devices are useless by themselves, but can be combined with others to create more effective means of securing property. I discovered that the price of the gadget didn't always mean it was better, as cheaper, simpler devices could be as useful, and at times rate the same on account of vulnerability. Some devices are popular because they are highly sophisticated, but may be as useful as having nothing installed at all.

A device that alerts you or local authority, by landline or mobile phone, whenever there is forced entry may cost a lot of money and promise a lot of security. But then all it takes to bypass this system is your phone line to be tapped, or cut, so that any outgoing calls from your house will be detected and rerouted, or blocked.

In most countries, law enforcement has been extensively infiltrated by stalker gangs, and the chance exists that the officer on duty when a distress call is made is connected to the stalkers. Sometimes, especially when the stalkers know such a system is installed, the arrival of law enforcement can be timed, even monitored by listening in on their frequencies, or by placing lookouts in strategic locations. If the intruders know they can gain entry and leave before law enforcement arrives, it will be the security system that will be put in question, and subsequent alarms may not receive a response. This security device is definitely useful when the criminal is not well connected, which most citizen harassers are.

The story is the same for high security locks, electronic or manual. Chances are that the combination key can be manipulated and entry gained into your premises, or that a master key or other device is already available that can easily turn the lock.

Electronic surveillance equipment is the best method of not only preventing illegal entry, but in instances of hidden cameras can provide proof of such entry, if not provide for a deterrent. You should however abstain from buying and merely installing such systems as they usually come with a lot of vulnerabilities as is. Systems with remote control capabilities are especially prone to remote manipulation. There are devices out there that can scan and replicate specific infrared signals used to operate such systems, which can then be used to disable alarms or unlock doors when the TI is not at home. There are devices that can blind motion sensors. A trained stalker may know of body movements impossible to pick up by motion sensors, and can literary tip-toe through a security installation relying on this technology.

The stalkers can also employ the brute force method, whereby they can gain access to the TI's property by dismantling whole entrances, manually neutralize alarm installations, and then proceed to record over video surveillance cameras in a manner that does not noticeably affect the time setting. They will then place everything back in place leaving no indicator there was forced entry.

The ability to rub out recordings and reset the setting of visual surveillance equipment is a major disadvantage especially when it works with timed inputs that can easily be rubbed back to zero and the owner will be non the wiser whether there has been entry or not, unless the equipment has logging capabilities whereby instances of entry are logged, and can be cross-checked with video footage. Such logging systems are however also prone to manipulation, unless they aren't easily accessible to intruders.

I do not want to put you off high-tech equipment. I am merely outlining the truth. As I said already, I learnt most of this the hard way. Most security systems are not always as secure as they are hyped up to be. They may be effective in certain situations, especially those involving common thieves who do not know better, but if the people after you are powerful enough, have sufficient connections in the right places, then you are better off following the advise I am giving.

Personalized/Sealed Security Systems

In the beginning, I placed a lot of expensive security systems on my doors and windows. At one time I had motion sensors installed on all entry points to my house. I had the best electronic surveillance equipment on the market, only to discover by a few tale tell signs left in my house that the stalkers were still managing to get in. I discovered over time that cheap, unconventional, home made contraptions were more effective at keeping such sophisticated gangs out of my property than their more expensive counterparts.

The first method that I used for some time involves continuous recording done by connecting a simple, cheap video camera to an old recorder with or without remote capabilities, and letting it run for the duration I was out. This method may not work for those who have to be away from home for periods longer than the capacity of their recording device, and entails timing the recording to prevent an intruder rubbing what has already been recorded, forcing him/her to act in a manner that reveals there was forced entry. Because I lived for some time off the proceeds of writing, I worked from my house, and could afford to stay indoors for prolonged periods, only going out for a few hours at a time to attend to some business.

This method involves quite a bit of constant reviewing of the tape every time you return, that isn't in itself lengthy given the advanced fast-forward capabilities of modern systems. Any video camera will do, that can also be connected to an alternative recording device. The camera does not necessarily have to be a surveillance type, though most surveillance cameras are cheaper, in fact much cheaper than a lot of conventional cameras, and come with features that you may find advantageous for other applications at the same low price; for example infrared and motion sensor capabilities. It is however not essential that you get a camera equipped with these extra features for this to work.

If your camera has no infrared capabilities, then leave the light turned on for the duration you are out, ensuring the light and camera are on a closed circuit. Ensure that the camera and the recorder, if any is attached, are well hidden. Placing the recorder in a well bolted closet is a good way of preventing it being taken away, or at least ensuring intruders work up a fearful sweat while they are at it. You should never make anything easy for them.

Start the recording as you are leaving, and verify everything is working by connecting a monitor or television that you turn and disconnect as soon as you verify this. The timing and sequence of this and the next activity alone will be your seal that should only be applied when your system does not have the capacity to record on screen displays of time and date.

Place a clock in front of the camera, preferably one that displays seconds to counter the possibility of a still image being projected to your recorder. Ensure it every number or hand is visible, otherwise adjust the focus. When reviewing your tape the time on the clock should be in sync with that on the recorder. Check your watch and record the time, and be off. Check the time when you return and verify that the length corresponds to the time the recording has lasted, then review the tape.
A system like this could be used when you live alone and do not go out much, or when you live with a family. In the latter case, it can be set to automatically start recording at the time when nobody is home, which can be useful in households where school children return at a certain time of day. This system has its flaws, but it is definitely more reliable than a similar recording device that utilizes high- tech automatic recording capabilities that can easily be manipulated without you knowing. If you can afford such equipment, then try to see whether you can figure out how it will be vulnerable. Talk to an expert on this if need be. Otherwise use it in combination with another system.

If this method is not for you, then you may consider sealing your locks. Sealing here means leaving a characteristic mark that cannot be altered or removed without breaking the seal. Ensure the seal you place on your lock cannot possibly be replaced with a similar one.

I started using personal seals when I was in situations where I could not afford to install surveillance equipment, especially when the stalking had become so brazen, when there were so many break-ins in the neighborhood that the possibility existed they could just force entry and take the equipment away. The loss is significantly less with a cheap lock, which also warns there has been unauthorized entry.

When I stumbled upon the idea of seals and started using them on my door, all signs of illegal entry and some physical symptoms disappeared immediately. Initially, after I had perfected this system to the point I became sure it could not be bypassed without leaving evidence, I noticed the stalkers had again started entering my space. My mental efforts were then turned into figuring out how they were bypassing what to me was a foolproof method of security, so that I could make it stronger.

The answer of how they were entering my property came to me accidentally when one day an entire window fell out as I leant into it. Closer scrutiny of the broken window revealed it had fallen out whole, hardened plaster included, and only broken as it hit the ground. The hardened plaster had come off in a clean manner, indicating it had been carefully pried loose so that the window could be removed and put back without leaving visible signs of entry. I verified the same with all windows large enough to allow a man through, after which I sealed them all from both the inside and out.

Soon after, things returned to normal.

The foolproof sealing method that drove my stalkers to dismantling entire window frames to gain entry into my property entailed placing a different loop each time around a medium sized, cheap lock strong enough not to be forced open without leaving signs. This loop, made from any kind of penetrable material that is impossible to cut, then stitch or glue back without leaving a sign, could not be removed when the lock was shut, could not be pushed aside to expose the keyhole without having to cut the material, and could also not be replaced with a replica without me knowing. I could however penetrate the material with a key, so that I was able to open my door, whereas if the lock was picked it would require making a hole in the looped material that would clearly be visible when I returned. This lock was placed on the inside of the door, and held in place by a chain attached to hoops whose screws were concealed under the metal to prevent tampering, so that access to it was through the normal lock on the door, making any attempt at replication difficult. Only people who knew how to pick locks could get to this second lock, which prevented the possibility an innocent visitor, even naughty child, may tamper with the lock.

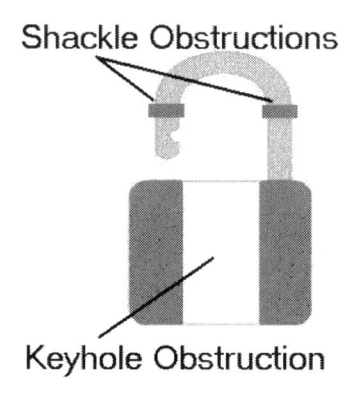

Shackle Obstructions

Keyhole Obstruction

This example shows a sealed padlock. This system may act as a deterrent but must be used in combination with locks and other security equipment that prevent forced entry as this is not what it is designed to do.

The shackle obstructions can either be made of metal welded in place and the characteristic shape or marks of and on this recorded or memorised. It can also consist of simpler material, for example tape, in which case a seal should be made on the material to alert of tampering.

The obstructions on the shackle are meant to prevent the insertion of objects through the gaps in the body, while the keyhole obstruction is designed to prevent picking of the lock. This has the advantage of being designed to fit, then put in place while the lock is open and, if properly made, can only be removed by tearing away, piercing or cutting.

The system may look simple, but it has alerted me of surreptitious entry on several occasions. The incursions only continued because the perps believed I was oblivious, and stopped completely when the reverse became apparent.

Keep in mind you are always closely monitored when under attack, so that your stalkers may observe that you have acquired surveillance equipment, or observe you installing it if they are using advanced technology to watch you within your own house. Unless you want it to serve as a deterrent, take all precautions not to alert them of any plans or traps you want to set, in your house or otherwise, because a few inquiries will reveal what kind of equipment you acquired, after which they will know whether they can bypass the security measures. If they only discover the fact while in your house, they will be forced to take action that reveals they were in your house, especially when they discover there is no way of concealing their presence. They may take the recording device with them, leaving only the evidence they were there, in which case you will have your first personal proof covert entry has been going on that, depending upon the level and history of crime in your area, may or may not be enough to prove to or alert necessary parties to what is happening.

When your stalkers cannot surreptitiously enter your home, they will realize you are playing the game on their terms. They will know they cannot wage and win a psychological war, and will be forced to use other tactics of attack. They may momentarily stop harassing you as they assess the situation, commit repeat break-ins in a show of force, or take the issue to a different level, of which regular and direct public verbal or physical confrontations or DEW are some.

You should always study the area you live in, and tailor your security measures to the circumstances. For example, if you live in a low population density area, an alarm would not be a very wise choice. It makes no sense having a noisy alarm when your next door neighbor cannot hear it, or when the only person who could hear the alarm is not always at home. An alarm would also not be a good idea in a noisy area where alarms always go off, or places where neighbors do not care about loud noises. High security measures are seldom the right solution for a house that is in a very busy location, especially when it's so situated that the system needs to be turned off to allow for coming and going.

Last Resort: the Mobile Home

Should the personalization method not work for you, then consider the method that involves actual carrying with you of articles known to be a favorite target for poisoning campaigns, aimed at gradual incapacitation that resembles natural disease.

Before I knew what the broken cylinder in the lock to my door meant, I was already suspicious people were entering my house and had long since started carrying personal belongings I considered crucial to my well-being in a backpack wherever I went, with the added precaution of washing my dishes thoroughly with detergent and cleaning utensils I would also neatly and air-tightly carry in my backpack. This also included the articles used in the long term, for example sugar, salt, some spices, toiletries like toothpaste, soap, etc. Such products are preferred for contamination because stalkers only have to sneak into a house every so often to achieve the equivalent of daily poisoning, as the victim will complete this task for them by administering a small portion each day, when brushing teeth, seasoning food.

You cannot buy a bag of salt, sugar, rice, toothpaste, etc., every day, but you can buy meat, chicken, soup, and such products on a daily basis, reducing the number of articles you need to carry around so that an average sized to small backpack is sufficient for the task. Ensure articles with odors are always encased in airtight containers. You do not want to attract that kind of attention to your person as it will only add to the stress.

Obviously, this method will entail a major change to the way you go about your daily life, without disrupting your life.

I was forced to stop doing the grocery on a weekly basis, and would only buy what I could consume till the next time I left the premises, which would mean evenings and mornings when I worked, Fridays when I planned to spend the weekend indoors. This also meant forcing myself to go to the shops whenever I needed to cook something I could not carry in my backpack. I kept this backpack with me wherever I went, never taking my eye off of it even when working. I can state with certainty that before I found a better method of securing my home, this method saved my life, and also provided for a lot of peace of mind. For example, discovery that my house had regularly, surreptitiously been broken into didn't come as a big shock that caused undue concern because I knew the damage they could have inflicted on my health, if they had wanted to, was limited.

The methods I provide above may be crude, or may not work for you, but it is crucial that you come up with original and foolproof methods of protecting yourself that are cheap but effective. It makes no sense hoping such attacks are not lethal, at least not in your case when a lot of evidence points to the fact damage to health is the main objective. Most targets are gradually killed by such attacks, society at large believing they succumbed from natural causes. Limiting lethal attacks to those launched remotely, for example DEW, is absurd since there are a lot of poisons or biological agents that can work as effectively, some of which can also not be detected in the blood, which in most cases would be an easier and more effective method of elimination.

This becomes truer when you realize the ease with which such groups can enter a victim's private property. Your very physical health, your very life is at stake. Your natural reaction should be the preservation of your life, which means utilizing any means necessary to prevent damage to your system, even if making it as difficult as you can for your stalkers is all you end up achieving. You owe yourself the peace of mind such activity brings, as this enables you to carry on with your life.

Chapter 6

Keeping Accounts

In This Chapter
▶ Poison Deposit Zones
▶ Other Personal Accounts

It is essential for a target of covert warfare to keep accounts of whatever transpires during the period, including the more difficult part of recording instances where actual attacks are identified. Keeping accounts serves to exonerate your own mental health to yourself in future. It may also be used to prove to others what really happened to you, and how long it has been going on.

Most attacks are aimed at destroying your mind. Once this is achieved you will find it difficult to stick to the truth as you knew it at a certain point. Some crucial experiences may get rubbed out of your memory. You might even lose the power of coherent thought, in which case it will be very difficult for you to reconstruct events from the past in a manner you, and crucially others, will find meaningful. This is exactly what you prevent from happening when you keep accounts.

Here, accounts should not be limited to visual and vocal recordings or writing, but to hair and nails where most poisons deposit.

Poison Deposit Zones

When your enemies want you eliminated, they will use any means at their disposal to achieve this objective. Poisons are not exempted from this, especially when they can gain access to your living space, contaminate the vents in your vehicle, or swap articles of shopping while you are not looking. Such poisons will usually deposit in your hair and nails. If you do not trust hospitals to help prove you are under attack, then keep these samples to send to any location or individual you feel you can trust, or simply keep them for the day you are in the clear. It is a good idea to stop the habit of constantly cutting hair, and let it grow for a while, then cut and store a small sample in an appropriate container, dating it appropriately. Results from tests of such samples will tell whether there has been attack with chemical agents, what you were attacked with and when. You can then use this to further your case against your stalkers.

Other Personal Accounts

If you have sufficient protection against DEW attacks, then your assailants will depend almost exclusively on chemical or biological agents to eliminate you, in which case they could start to pump dangerous substances into your living environment. Such attacks will mostly not register in the same sudden manner known in cases of food poisoning, but will gradually destroy you from the inside out, manifesting as systemic failure when the damage has reached a critical point.

Indicators your environment is being polluted with harmful substances include experiencing a burning sensation at the back of your throat when in your house, a sudden high tone of voice, chest pains that only occur when you are in your home, a reduction of the depth of your chest and size of your neck while the rest of your body stays the same, sudden, extreme fatigue that you only experience in one location, etc.

Symptoms of disease caused by such attacks are dependent on the agents used and individual reactions to them, but could include loss of libido, pain in the joints, and nausea. When you identify these problems as emanating or worsening while you are in your house, find out whether there is no gas leak or something similar causing this, after which you will have to keep the interior as clean as you can. If this doesn't stop the problem, then find out whether the same is the case when you spend time out of the house.

Sleep at a friends house, ensuring this is a friend your assailants do not know about, a visit they could not have predicted, or make a one off booking at a hotel in the city. Check your state before you go to sleep, and when you awake in the morning. Remember here that some effects from poisoning take time to disappear, so that a single day in the clear may not be sufficient for decisive results, though if you are under attack in your own house, on a daily basis, some symptoms will become very clear.

If you wake up breathing better, refreshed, feeling and looking much better, if all the symptoms experienced in your own house were not as severe, then you can be sure you are being gassed in your own home. Moving out is a must, and should be done as soon as possible, but if you remain in reach of your stalkers then the relief you will experience by relocation will be short lived since they will be scrambling to get to you in the new location. They know the changes caused to your appearance in the new location will have you and others suspicious. They have to keep you behaving or looking a certain way, so eventually, they will simply set up shop in your new location and the nightmare will start all over again.

Keep written and recorded accounts of your experiences, making it a point to go through especially the writing as often as possible, to update the accounts where necessary. This refreshes your memory, and keeps your linguistic and coherency skills at par. You keep track of yourself, remaining in touch with how your mind worked and how you perceived your surroundings, which is useful in gauging how much your mind was or has been affected.

To such accounts should be added pictures, especially those that clearly show deterioration. When you are successfully fighting off covert attacks, your stalkers will usually notice this by changes in your appearance, and will step up their attacks accordingly. A cat and mouse game will ensue whereby you will observe the physical symptoms of attack come and go each time you also step up your security, and they step up the offensive. These ups and downs will clearly be visible on your pictures, and will provide you with evidence of what you were going through; never mind such an experience is one most people would like to put behind should the day come for freedom from the torture.

The reactions people make to your state will tell how you are faring regarding attacks or measures against attacks at a particular moment in time, so that they will not be able to give you a fuller picture of recovery or degeneration over the long term. Pictures and video recordings are more useful as they can be preserved over long periods of time, telling much more than the occasional encounter with a stranger or even a known person can.

Also know that your idea of how you look is determined by your actual state, just like your general state of mind determines your level of understanding. You are as unlikely to notice deterioration in your physical state as you are to notice mental decline. You get used to how you look at a moment in time, and will be surprised images that looked normal to you are in fact not so in retrospect, especially in cases when your general health has improved significantly.

Chapter 7

Securing your Home

In This Chapter
▶ **Contaminants on Solid Articles**
▶ **Airborne Attacks**

Covert attacks on the suspecting or unsuspecting can be opportunistic or planned, meaning they can be chance attacks launched when the victim wanders into a situation that exposes them to danger, or when movements of the target are anticipated so that an ambush is prepared for them. Highly mobile individuals with tight schedules in different locations are highly susceptible to the latter kind of attacks. Pre-booked hotel accommodation or transportation can be contaminated in anticipation of the target's arrival.

Such attacks are however highly risky especially since their success depends on a number of factors coming together, mostly dependent on the whim of the target, or others within the immediate area. Hotel bookings or car hires can be cancelled. If the owner of the hotel or hire vehicle is not aware of the attack plan, they could allot the room or rent the car to another individual who would in turn suffer exposure to whatever was planned for a totally different person.

Upon release from prison, I had lost my accommodation and ended up at a Salvation Army homeless shelter. I was made to understand this was the location of last resort. I was not at fault, but my rehabilitation worker had neglected to plan ahead of my release. I would soon discover the outcome was far from negligence on the part of this rehabilitation worker, but that it was planned.

The first sign of this was an unusually high level of recognition from the residents at the center when I arrived, and a lot of statements were made to that effect every time I would walk past some groups of individuals.

That night, I felt the onset of a fever as I attempted to sleep, and soon my condition worsened to the extent I soon found myself gasping for air. The symptoms disappeared as soon as I left the bed area and took a walk around the halls of the center. I spent that night spread out on chairs set side by side in the dining room where I could at least breathe properly, discovering in between that the symptoms returned as soon as I attempted to get into my bed.

I could not claim contamination of the bedding the next day, as nobody would have believed the bed had anything to do with the sudden health crisis, which would have resembled the normal process of a fever where the patient hangs between feeling too hot and too cold, but I managed to get a different bed in a different room by lodging a real and opportune complaint against a nasty room mate. I had the fortune of being placed in the same room with a fellow I became convinced was well aware of covert warfare. He was as paranoid; in fact much more paranoid than I was, so that he spent his time in the center with his eye perpetually on the room. The reason he gave for this was that there was a lot of theft in the building.

I slept well that night, and the next few nights I spent at the center, before I left for the streets after I realized it was too dangerous here.

A few days after this incident, a new arrival to the center was placed in my former bed. Residents in the center woke up that night to the sound of an ambulance siren that had been called when the new resident had suddenly fallen seriously ill in the middle of the night. I would later learn that he had suffering from the same symptoms I had, only worse in his case. Apparently, even a change of bedding had not been able to protect him from whatever had been sprayed on that bed.

This unpredictability in targets or the behavior of those around has the potential to expose such plots, and is the reason the vast majority of attacks tend to be concentrated on the home of the target, where the entire place can be contaminated or the habits of the target in their home studied, eliminating as such the chance somebody else falls victim to what is meant for another.

Home is also the place where we spend the most time out of our lives, where we are conveniently isolated, the place where we engage in activities that make it possible for our very life to go on. We spend two fifths of our time inside our homes, if we include the period before and after sleep, that takes an average of a third of the time. We prepare and eat food, sleep, bath, prepare for the next day within our homes.

Contaminants on Solid Articles

Of all activities carried out in our homes, the one that is indispensable to the location is sleep. We may be able to eat out for as long as it takes, may be able to lunch at a local restaurant, or at a friends or relative's house, may be able to take a bath when visiting, or regularly at the local gym, but then the most we can do in these locations where sleep is concerned is nap, if not have a one night sleep over.

Normally, you require to give a good reason for wanting to lodge for a prolonged period at another person's house, especially in cases where you already have your own place. In instances where a target is fleeing from covert stalking, this reason will have to be made up since the majority of the population does not believe covert warfare of this nature exists. If the TI does manage to contrive an excuse and move in, then as soon as this new location becomes permanent, it becomes the TI's home too and will sooner or later be subject to covert attacks.

Scientific research reveals the average person sleeps not so much to recuperate from the day's activities, considering the meager average of 50 KCal that is saved overall, but more to maintain normal levels of cognitive skills like speech, memory, innovative and flexible speech. This ties brain development itself to the activity. This premise is easily proven by the fact lack of sleep is known to have serious effects on the brain's capacity to function. Anyone who has gone for long periods without sleep may know of side effects that result like grumpiness, short attention span and reduced ability to concentrate. Apart from impacting on cognitive functioning, lack of sleep is known to cause physical disorders such as sleep apnoea. This causes excessive daytime sleepiness and has been linked to high blood pressure or stress.

The role sleep plays in our mental health is the reason most harassers make it a point to disrupt the sleep of a target, either by noisy displays at ungodly hours, or using all manner of DEW weapons to prevent sleep. Some victims have reported waking up at the same time every night, a very strong indicator they are being kept awake by remote attacks.

Though common sense dictates you keep away from your home when under this level of attack, the ability to stay away is restricted by factors peculiar to each individual, and by the role sleep plays in our mental and physical well-being for all cases. As long as the amount of sleep an individual gets by utilizing the social network is insufficient, they will sooner or later find it imperative to get back to their home to catch up on the sleep they have missed, and will do so irregardless the home is virtually haunted, as the need to sleep will override security concerns. This means taking the risk of waking up an altered person the next day, which could mean being in a more vulnerable mental state so that taking the necessary precautions becomes progressively harder. Depending on the effect the attacks have had on the victim and his surroundings, it may become impossible for some targets to stay away from home for prolonged periods, leading in many cases to a situation whereby the victim finds leaving the house almost impossible.

If you cannot find an alternative sleeping place, resist the temptation to leave at all costs, which could mean sleeping in hotels or sleeping rough, moving from place to place. This reaction is natural, but you should know you are safer sleeping in your own home and coping with the attacks than going out into the unknown. Remember that even when you are out in the open you remain susceptible to the very body functions that make you vulnerable in your own home. When the need to sleep takes over in your home, you are at least between the safety of your four walls, whereas if it takes over while you are in shared room accommodation, for example, or sleeping rough, you are that much more vulnerable to attack since your very body is exposed.

Unless you have the energy to keep on the move during the night, a newbie to rough sleeping is a sitting duck for covert attacks, and the effects of attacks while sleeping rough can be much more severe than those experienced while inside. I know this because I spent some time sleeping rough. It makes a lot of sense therefore that you never consider the option of leaving your house, no matter how intolerable the attacks get, unless you are sure you will be safe.

Going out every now and then to refresh the senses, staying out as long as is possible, then returning to gain some sleep, is a much better option to abandoning the house for the streets.

TI's are always outnumbered by stalkers, who will include other homeless people they meet, and their movements can always be anticipated. The streets, including hotels and hostels, are by design run by stalker groups, who know every corner well. This is not to imply owners of hotels or hostels are always in on the conspiracy, but out of personal experience and accounts from other people, I know these places usually have their own stalker denizens. This appears to have become a necessity in most western countries.

I spent a long time running in and out of hotels, and when I could not afford these then I would resort to hostels. Normally, I would have a few days of rest before all hell broke loose, after which the stalkers would literally take over the hostel. It only took one of their kind to get a bed in the same room before the others would flood in and cause all manner of disturbances. Hostels would usually be full of tourists who would prevent the stalkers launching attacks during the night. This forced them to resort to loud displays that would last throughout the night, intensifying when I would attempt to sleep.

In shared rooms, it is easy for a member of a stalking gang to get a bed next to a target since all they have to do is pay a fee at the reception. If one does not get the bed next to the TI the first time, then another will.

Stay in your home, thus. The most important thing to do is ensure your personal space cannot be violated. When your house is not secure, unless in cases where the attacks are non-lethal, your food, your sitting places, your bed, your shower, indeed everything in the house is game for contamination, so that you are denied the basic life comforts this place is meant to provide. As already mentioned before, the most common avenue of attack is through food that you use in every meal, for prolonged periods, for example salt, sugar, cooking oil, spices, and such, or toiletry articles like toothpaste, shampoo or soap that are also used for prolonged periods.

These articles are a favorite for such attacks because it ensures the continuous supply of poisons to your system. A bag of sugar once contaminated will be consumed with various other foods: tea, coffee, and some foods, over a period ranging from a week to a month, depending on the consumption habit and size of the bag. A one off contamination ensures a steady supply of poisons to your body. The advantage for the stalkers is also that they do not need to enter your premises on a daily basis to recontaminate the articles you previously replaced because they know you will do the contamination yourself, which can be useful when your house is almost perpetually habited, or the street in which you live is almost always watched by neighbors.

In cases where you live with other people, the attack methods change for fear of contaminating the entire household, which could raise eyebrows. Instead, time is spent studying the victim to know what perfumes he uses, what his/her favorite clothes are, etc. Stalkers will then select through the wardrobe or toiletries for objects that belong to the target, an easy thing when the man or woman is a parent in a family where the rest are children. Such contamination is also similar to the previous method in that it guarantees a steady exposure to harmful substances. If, for example, the victim shaves, then the exposure will last as long as the shaving cream lasts. When the victim uses a cream, then the harmful substance is rubbed in with every application.

If you cannot keep the door to your house safely locked, then try the method outlined previously of taking vital articles with you.

You should always ensure your environment is spot clean. You should wash and refresh articles of clothing as often as possible. Carpets should be regularly vacuumed, the living environment aired regularly. Working tables should be wiped thoroughly before use.

Though the floor and walls of your own house can be sprayed or smeared with substances that cause illness, they are not a very good choice for such attacks because these surfaces can be cleaned, or tend to clean out with certain activities. Walls can get covered with moisture from perspiration or cooking, that has the potential to dilute the poisons used, rendering them ineffective. This reality should not make you get lazy with the exercise of daily vacuuming or dusting.

What also requires special attention are the articles you use regularly such as your cooking pots and related utensils and the substances you use to clean them; places where you spend the most time while in your house such as your sofa, more especially your bed, at times even when you share it with another person. To this can also be added the clothes and shoes you like to wear. Like the seasoning and other substances you always add to your food and drinks, bedding once contaminated may prevent you from having a good night's sleep until the next time you do the laundry. This contamination only needs to be done once, ensuring that the administering of the poisons is repeated every time you go to sleep, every time you put on your favorite jacket or shoes, until the next time you throw these into the washing machine, or the poisons wear out in the case of shoes.

From personal experience of such attacks, some of the substances used can induce fever, while those used in shoes cause cramp, making it difficult to walk. I remember times I would wake up feeling very feverish, sweating profusely even on a cold day, attracting attention when I would board a bus and start sweating while everyone was wearing thick coats to protect against the cold. These sweat attacks every morning would be short lived, unlike the case would be with a fever caused by an infection, lasting an hour or so after waking up. I would completely be cured by the time it was afternoon, looking considerably better than when I had walked into the working place.

I noticed that I did not have the same symptoms as soon as I washed and slept in clean sheets. Unfortunately, the symptoms would return a few days thereafter. They disappeared completely when I installed foolproof security methods, including the means to keep my space secure from invasion by DEW weapons.

The place where I discovered and verified this form of attack was prison, the one place it is virtually impossible to fight off. Initially, though I was physically strong, seldom sick and engaged regularly in sports, it was difficult to have a good night's sleep, and I always woke up feeling very feverish. Soon enough, the condition caused a real change to my appearance, prompting and justifying the guards to place me alongside other inmates with conditions and afflictions, in the cells nearest to their offices where they could keep an eye on us.

I still have pictures that show how I looked before going into prison, and others while I was in prison. I never did anything different while I was imprisoned that I did not do while free, so there was no logical explanation for the sudden deterioration in appearance, especially the fact I improved immediately after release, even though I ended up homeless.

I had already been a target of covert attacks while on the outside so I already had my guard raised in prison. I suspected from the symptoms I was getting that I was being drugged, and was on the lookout for the source. One day, despite an unstable mental state, I had the presence of mind to notice I woke up feeling refreshed only after fresh washing of my bedding, but only at times when I had kept my washing watched. This coincided with a period of thefts from the floor's washing machine that prompted guarding of clothes.

The next day, after the day's activities when cell blocks are vacated by prisoners in turns, a period of the day when it is impossible to keep an eye on personal property, depending on the guards who had duty (and I believe most were in on the conspiracy), I would not sleep nor wake up feeling as well as the first time, even though my bedding was still clean, having only been used once.

It was unfortunately impossible to pinpoint who the culprit was. It could have been prison guard(s) or a fellow prisoner because cells were sometimes opened while some occupants were out, and were regularly searched for drugs, weapons, or signs of activity connected to security. Neither could I report the case to authority as nobody would have believed this version of events. What most people would have thought was that I was mistaking symptoms. I could therefore only rely on washing my sheets and clothes to protect myself.

As these events were unfolding, a few of the prisoners started the same habit seen by stalkers on the outside of throwing statements at me when they passed me by. I was particularly reminded on an almost daily basis "I would never get out of this one" again, meaning I had already got out of situations I was not aware of.

Since it is impossible to wash sheets on a daily basis in prison, the best I could do was air them before I slept in them. I started wearing a track suite and T-shirt under my clothes that I would sleep in, using for a pillow any garment or object I ensured could not be contaminated in the same manner. This way, I avoided direct contact with the bedding. Noteworthy here is the fact the period I slept in clean sheets ensured I didn't experience night sweats, even when I went to bed all dressed, so that there was reduced conduction for whatever substance my bedding was contaminated with.

I also ensured that all surfaces were constantly wiped clean. This had very visible effects apart from the mere fact I felt much stronger and refreshed whenever I woke up. In fact, I moved rapidly from being the sickly looking prisoner who was nonetheless much stronger and muscled than most others, back to the normal looking prisoner with the same qualities. Of course, the other inmates had had their own suspicions before this change in appearance occurred for the simple reason the two do not mix (heavily muscled and strong but sickly looking), but they got even more suspicious after the change back to the original.

I had proven to myself that the harassing I was a victim of on the outside had followed me into jail, that I had in most probability been arrested for that reason, especially since I was capable of evading serious injury when free, but it was hard to convince other inmates of this since this world is usually beyond the average citizen's imagination. They were suspicious alright, but their suspicion was more confusion than anything else since the majority were simply in a state where they could not make sense of what they were seeing.

Of course I could not reveal the methods I was using to protect myself because I couldn't know who was listening. Rather, I attempted to tell select individuals what I had experienced outside prison, and how I managed to survive those attacks. They sadly equated the situation to phone tapping, plain clothed police surveillance, and such; anything within the realm of their imagination other than the obscure or unknown reality whistleblowers and activists are considered bigger threats to a government or corporation than some violent robber driving around in a Mercedes, making his next robbery plans.

Otherwise they wondered how important I was socially, since in their imagination only the visibly high ranking qualified for what they interpreted as high level surveillance. When I pushed the issue, they would normally ask why law enforcement or a government would be bothered about the activities of an average citizen when drug barons and all manner of criminals were running around, committing high level crimes.

One thing people cannot understand is how a man or woman who has been under the kind of attack described in these stories can still possess the capacity of coherent thought, let alone be alive. Survivors and others who continue to be victims of covert warfare are denied the verity of their story only on account of the fact they can still think, talk, and are still alive. The assumption is therefore that any person who gets attacked in this manner should be an idiot or dead.

As usual, I was alone in this, a survivor whose account could not even be taken for consideration, and in my mind I could see the psychotics behind such torture crack a wide smile of delight. The best I could keep doing was defend myself against covert attacks, which at that time included not letting the guards who checked on us throughout the night realize what I was doing. I managed to pull it off for the duration, but it was a tedious procedure, not only because of the difficulty in concealing, but also because ensuring I had a clean set of clothes the next day meant washing my clothes every evening. The plan was usually put in disarray by unforeseen events like long visits by friends, sudden removal from the cell to attend to some business by the authorities that left my washed clothes unattended, without sufficient time to rewash and dry them again. This meant wearing dirty clothes at moments when this was not the best thing to do.

This came to pass when I discovered a better method of avoiding exposure to agents put in my bedding. By rolling a clean sheet into a tight cylindrical shape, it became small enough to place into a money bag, so that I could carry it with me throughout the day, even when doing sports. I would unroll it at night when it was time to go to bed.

Stalkers will always monitor their target carefully, on a daily basis to verify their attacks are having the desired effects. They will adjust the intensity or nature of the attack when they see changes in the state of the victim that are not in line with expectations. If a target looks better than they should under the circumstances, the attack method will either be intensified or changed. Everything will be done to ensure the symptoms return, and stay.

Stalkers need to be sure they are inflicting damage. They need something to show for their activities otherwise they do not get the breaks those who put them up to such activities promised. Maintaining a state in a target that looks progressive also helps maintain in the community the idea the individual merely has an affliction, an opinion hard to alter due to the current mentality where people believe in shying away from physical conditions, or wear different clothes each day so that they cannot be identified as the person who looked weak the previous day.

These successful methods of keeping myself safe in prison had to be augmented with other methods because the intensity of attacks would always be raised as soon as it became apparent the current method was not bearing desired results.

Airborne Attacks

If perpetrators have moved in next to you, there is the real possibility they could start pumping harmful biological or chemical agents into your living environment. Wearing gas masks in your own house may be out of question, but consider this option when the situation gets out of hand.

I should not say this lightly, because I know it is almost impossible for people who are not protecting themselves against attacks to know when they are under attack, let alone when it gets out of hand. Usually, the effects from such substances take hold slowly, insidiously, so that the victim gradually starts to take their physical state for granted. Only when a TI mounts full and effective protection will they notice how much they have been under attack. This unfortunately means they will usually only know when they are under attack, or when it is out of hand, when they have kept their system away from harmful substances long enough for the mind to be refreshed enough to register such change.

Having an air filtering system is a very good way of ensuring you are supplied with fresh air while you are in your home. Make sure the flow of fresh air from the outside into your house is uninterrupted, but also that it is unidirectional, without it turning into a draft. This means the air you breathe should be moving in through the front or back window, and moving out a different vent in your room/house. This maintains a flow of uncontaminated air into your living environment, a simple method of ensuring whatever contaminants pumped into your living space are promptly pumped out.

Find out the possible vulnerable spots or people around you who are involved in the attacks to be sure of the direction airborne attacks may come from. Let fresh air move into your house and exit in the direction you suspect air contamination could come from. Place your sofa or bed closest to the fresh air supply. Avoid using for air inlet windows accessible to the general public by touch or within throwing distance, only opening those that are out of reach of anyone. Be aware that stalkers may gain access to these inlets too when nobody is watching.

When you open a window that has been sprayed with some harmful substance, you will let the dangerous fumes into your house. Some of these substances can last for long periods so that contamination of your atmosphere will occur every time you open the window. Make it a point to regularly wash the exterior and interior of these air inlet points, using rubber gloves to avoid direct exposure to substances that might have been put there.

I still carry around pictures I took of my backyard where it is clearly evident that an otherwise healthy tree standing directly outside my window withered only on the side closest to my window. In this picture can clearly be seen the damage done to this tree, and can be compared to the state of the same kind of tree growing a few meters away from this first tree, that is growing much more evenly and healthily than the other. I took the photos after nights when I would hear liquids being poured outside. I was forced to seal that particular window when I noticed that I got noxious fumes instead of fresh air whenever I would open it, even after I had thoroughly cleaned it.

Cleaning this particular window in the winter when the tree was bare of leaves had always provided for fresh air into my bedroom. But then in the winter it is too cold to always open windows. Since it was autumn, coming on to summer, there was a need to open windows more, therefore more cleaning was required, but then clean as I may, I could only get fresh air by walking out of the house because the air that came in through the window remained oppressive.

It was autumn so there was no need to use the kind of heating that might be blamed for the effect seen on the tree, nothing I was doing in my house that would have caused the damage to the tree that my neighbor, who also had the same tree in front of his window, was not doing. The damage seen on the tree was clearly deliberate spraying of a substance whose poisonous fumes would be drawn into my living atmosphere, the effect of which had caused the tree to die on one side.

Actually, this was not the first time I had been exposed to this method of attack.

Like all prisoners, I had undergone extensive and compulsory tests upon entry into the institution, which had revealed there was nothing wrong with my lungs, which was also evident in my endurance capacities when engaging in strenuous activities, such as playing football or body building. Looking good, having above average strength and size, and having endurance of course meant dealing with more intensified attacks.

Though I occasionally relapsed into looking a mess, my strength was obviously an indicator to my stalkers that I was not being affected to the extent they wanted. The visible sign of the attack in how disoriented and imbalanced I was would however have put them off increasing attack intensity since they would have believed my body would be worn down eventually. Clear signs of recovery threw this theory in disarray.

Shortly after I had taken care of the bed incidents, they decided for another channel of attack. The very air I breathed in my cell began to get contaminated by either the smearing of substances onto the furniture in the cell that released poisonous fumes into the air, or through an entry point I have to date not established. This was so evident I did not need to make any trials to ascertain the reality. A simple walk into the cell from the day's activities, that included two hours of fresh air, would be as oppressive to the senses as it would be to my mental health, since it was on this level that I dealt with the reality of spending a night in a space that was killing me. This foul, contaminated environment was not obvious during the day when all cells are opened and prisoners are allowed to move around freely, the time when most of the cleaning and tidying up was done. It seeped in slowly, soon after the doors were closed shut for the day, when nobody could accidentally walk in.

On the inside, I could feel the changes that indicated the methods and weapons being used in attack had changed, that the new agent was different. I was no longer prone to feverish attacks, but rather felt drunk, disoriented, forgetful, completely out of my body. Any rhythmic activity, including music, stopped making sense, so that I would no longer be able to respond to familiar beats. My balance and timing was also severely affected, so that though I had the strength and stamina, I could not play any sport to previous levels. This change was clearly evident to other prisoners, and they were quick to let me know. For example, I moved from being a player whose style would always get compared to one or other famous footballer, to the guy nobody wanted to pass the ball to, so that doing sports in a group became a torturous affair.

The cells had air inlets above the window that let fresh air in. These were about a meter wide, the width of the window, and about three fingers or centimeters high. There was a wire mesh within the space to prevent small objects being passed through. This little hole was insufficient for air supply, hence the air ventilation system via vents on top of each cell door whose suction let air in from the outside, and also from the hall through the gap at the bottom of the door.

By sealing the gap at the base of the door with a towel every evening, I prevented the ventilation system from sucking in air from the hall in between cells that would not be fresh enough, forcing in fresh air from the outside, through the air inlets above the window that I cleaned out every evening. Wearing plastic gloves or any non-porous material, I wiped all surfaces of the cell clean with the interior cleaner supplied for every prisoner, ensuring I followed directives so as not to contaminate the environment again with the very cleaner, soaping everything from tables, chairs, to the oil paint walls.

The effect of religious dedication to these simple measures was as obvious as they were immediate. But then as soon as I was getting my personality back, the ventilation system itself started going on and off each day, every time it would go off bringing the sense of being swamped with foul, harmful air back. Soon after this, the system broke down completely. I knew I was in the worst position any person would want to be in when the system stayed broken even after prisoners had complained and a mechanic had come around to fix it. The period stretched on from a single day to a week, and each day after activities I would walk into my cell wondering whether I would walk out alive the next day.

Air in a prison is oppressive enough as it is, but when the central ventilation system stopped working it became so bad it was obvious even to the most untidy of prisoners.

I found that I fared better when I would keep a sheet over my head through the night, or kept breathing through a moist piece of cloth placed over my nose, acting as a gas mask, for as long as possible, even though this reduced the body's overall air intake. I was at a loss, fearing for the worst, when one day I came upon an idea. I used the fan in my cell to pump the foul air out of my cell and into the hall onto which all prison cells opened. I achieved this by wrapping plastic around the fan creating a cylinder that I taped to the base of the door where there was a gap. Once turned on, the fan acted as an air pump, sucking air through the plastic cylinder shape and out through the base of the door into the hall.

It worked! Soon enough, the air in my cell was refreshed with fresh air from the outside. I slept well that night, and woke up feeling even better, but noticed with dismay that the other prisoners had not fared as well at all that night. They exhibited the same symptoms that so often weighed me down, the ones I kept close intimating they felt dizzy and disoriented.

Nowhere was this state more obvious than during sport. We had sport that afternoon; I didn't participate, but stayed indoors and watched the game of football from my window. It became at once apparent that the poor prisoners were much more disoriented than I had ever been while under the influence, failing to get their aim strait at every turn. In frustration, with an element of complaint and indignation, the prisoners directed their rage at the ball, kicking it about wildly in a display never before seen on this pitch.

To this day, I chide myself for having laughed out loud at what was not a funny display at all. I also got insight into my physical strength.

Prisoners are never quiet about disturbances to their sleep. Had they noticed anything foul during the night, they would have made it plain by banging on the walls and making all manner of noises. Most of them stated clearly they had slept well and not noticed anything different at all during the night. The air in prison at that particular time had become foul enough as it was. Adding onto that foulness the air from one cell would hardly have made a difference. As I said already, some stated they felt dizzy and disoriented that morning. In confirmation of this, that day, there was a resurgence of talk of food contamination from the usual, cynical corners.

It's essential here that I make you understand the dimensions of the prison block so you can assess the situation yourself, to even see why I came to wonder at my strength.

There were a roll of 25, 2 meter (width of wall included) wide cells on each side, two rows high, and a cooking space for all at the end added 10 meters to the length of the block. This means the hall was at least 60 meters long. The cells were approximately 3.5 meters in length, two and a half meters high, and the hall between the cells was a good 25 meters wide and, by adding the heights of each cell plus spaces between, plus the dome shape at the top, at least 8 meters high. We had a pool table, two table tennis tables, and a seating area for 20 prisoners at a time in the hall. Inmates could occupy all game tables, while others sat and watched, and there would be enough room for all. Yet I observed and was told of dizziness and disorientation by prisoners whose cells were 10 or so removed from mine.

Soon after this incidence, the air ventilation system was finally permanently fixed so that it was no longer necessary to ventilate the room by any other means. Constant cleaning of the air inlets, maintenance of the cloth changing regime, and other activities ensured that I stayed strong and healthy of body and mind until the time I was released from prison. Incidentally, my experiences in prison were confirmed by total strangers, while others used the experience to threaten me of worse to come if I didn't stop writing.

I owe knowledge of this reality to the measures I took to ascertain cause (testing things out), and also the fact my stalkers became emboldened enough to openly reveal to me what they had or were doing to me, due in part to panic at the realization I was fending off attacks that necessitated stronger methods of attrition, and in part due to their belief they would eventually completely get away with it. In many ways they did, and will continue to get away with such cases given the record to date, as long as this reality is not brought into the imagination of the average citizen.

Chapter 8
Blocking Directed Energy Weapons

In This Chapter
► History
► How DEW's Work
► Obstruction

Directed Energy Weapons are a favorite choice for stalkers in covert warfare because they leave no characteristic mark that points to their use, especially when the exposure is low level, aimed at inducing discomfort on the long term. When the victim's health starts to ail, when they develop conditions known to result from long term exposure to harmful electromagnetic beams, the affliction itself gets the blame for the bad state of health or resulting death. A victim may get cancer and succumb to it, and everyone will think it was a naturally occurring cancer that caused their demise.

Since elimination is not always achieved using DEW alone, but can also involve chemical or biological agents, there are times when it can be confusing for the target themselves to know whether the manifesting symptoms are caused by exposure to DEW or not. For example, both exposure to microwave radiation and heavy metal poisoning can result in nausea, blurred vision, pain in the joints, impairment of the body's immune system, extreme fatigue, etc., in which case the after-effect would not indicate to the target whether they were attacked with DEW or not.

There are undoubtedly people who would be attacked with DEW, who would feel the discomfort at the time of exposure, for example needle like pain in a part of the body, or painful warming up of organs, but would not know unless they were told that this indicates an actual DEW attack. There are people who experience constant ringing in the ears consistent with that created when a target is being bombarded with harmful beams of a given wavelength, but would not recognize this as the DEW attack that it is, unless they were told.

Fortunately, some DEW attacks are easily discerned, especially due to the electrical nature of the sensations. But then there are a lot more symptoms with which the majority needs to be familiarized before they can recognize attacks.

Below are some indicators of exposure to DEW bombardment:

- Constant ringing in the ears when in certain environments. This can come in various pitches, can be constant or intermittent, and can occur in both or only one ear. The sound may manifest as a low rumbling noise or the high pitch of a small motor, for example a hair cutter. A mere feeling of discomfort may accompany the noise, while at other times it could be excruciatingly painful.

- Unnatural fast movement from an adverse to a normal state of health, especially when it follows the victim's movements. Some targets report feeling sick at home only, feeling better when they go out.

- Clicking noises inside the sinuses or ears.

- Manipulation of body parts, especially involuntary pulsing or contracting of muscles. Feet, legs, arms, and individual fingers can be made to move by sudden jerking or the motion can be slow and controlled. Most of this often occurs in one location, at night in bed.

- Piercing sensation on the skin. This involves a mild or painful feeling that the skin is being pierced by a needle.

- Heating of internal organs. This usually involves a sensation whereby the internal organs feel like they are being heated up from the inside out. This experience is mostly connected to one locality, though it can happen anywhere.

- Some victims report suffering from sinus problems. This can be very painful and agitating, with the sinuses filling up and pulsing, often preventing sleep from occurring.

- Sensation of having genitalia manipulated. Both men and women report this. It involves tingling, prickling, arousal and/or pain of the genital area. It is a particularly disturbing experience. This isn't by any stretch a "natural" occurrence, given the "artificial/electronic" nature of the sensation.

- Tapping or Banging noises that can be several sounds, or involve a singular, sudden tap or bang just as the person is falling asleep, waking them immediately. The sounds may be experienced as coming from the outside environment.

- Waking up at exactly the same time every night. This may or may not be due to the tapping sound described above. The factor distinguishing this as a DEW attack is that it is physically impossible for a healthy person to wake up at exactly the same time of night, irregardless of their sleep routine.

- Experiencing erratic activity in electronic appliances whereby they operate in unpredictable or inexplicable ways. Machinery containing motors will run far too fast, and/or far too loud, causing them to break down quickly.

- About half of targeted people hear voices, often identified to be those who are perpetrating the crime. The technology exists to transmit sound inside peoples heads, bypassing the ears altogether. There is speculation that this is a form of microwave hearing. Some report hearing the voices outside of their heads, as though there is a speaker inside their home somewhere.
- Some report visual hallucinations. Seeing colored lights is commonly reported.

- Many people experience a racing or pounding heart just as they are about to go to sleep.

- "Pseudo" heart attacks. This involves the sensation that the chest is being tightly constricted, mimicking the symptoms of a heart attack.

- Other symptoms could include social isolation, chronic fatigue and other illnesses, headaches, thoughts of suicide, depression, inability to hold a job, diagnoses of mental illness, and such.

I do not intend to provide a false sense of security, but the most important thing you should know before you read on is it is possible to protect yourself from all types of DEW attacks. It is an established fact that all frequencies have vulnerabilities, and the methods I will present provide tested ways of obstruction of a group of frequencies at a time. When these various methods are used in combination, they suffice to make a location impenetrable to all DEW attacks.

Specialized knowledge is necessary to implement some of these methods, but shortcut measures are also available for those who do not have either the specialized knowledge, or cannot make the changes required to the interior and/or afford prices that come with some obstructions.

By shortcut measures I mean those that can be applied with ease, using material available to anyone, available in retail outlets everywhere. These are materials that can be painted over or covered and will not be visible to visitors. Most of this material is familiar because it is used daily in households, a good example being insulation foil used in construction, or simple kitchen foil that when applied in sufficient layers can block out the most harmful of microwaves. Aluminum foil can be pasted onto a wall in layers, then covered with wallpaper. Aluminum wallpaper or metalized paint is also available at a number of searchable retail outlets.

The shortcut methods offer good, though non comprehensive protection. This level of protection when combined with other measures is adequate to provide for sufficient relief from effects of harmful beam exposure to allow the victim to engage ever more effectively in activities that impact positively on their situation. This can also include learning or taking the time to install the more complex methods.

In order to cope with the reality the obstructions that are successful (especially by measuring the amount of relief they give once applied) will eventually be overridden because the attack groups spend a lot of time and money searching for frequencies and frequency-combinations that do not have current vulnerabilities, I will give the amount of protection necessary for complete obstruction in each case. For example, a layer of foil on the wall where attacks are suspected to be coming from will give a degree of protection, but the stalkers could easily turn the power of the magnetron higher, bypassing this protection. 6 layers of aluminum foil will provide sufficient protection for handheld, and most microwave devices that can be carried in cars or into households.

A layer of overlapping sheet metal is unsightly, but will block out even the most powerful of microwaves, whereas the number of layers of foil will have to be increased to cope with the same increase in power. Twelve layers of aluminum foil is sufficient to block out military grade equipment that is in itself too large to be carried in a medium sized car, let alone be carried through a normal household door. Informed sources indicate a portable magnetron powerful enough to harm a large group of demonstrators, for example; would require space equal to a small truck. Such powerful equipment is actually normally only found at military installations, and unless you suspect your stalkers will go to the extent of carrying such a device to your front door, the standard advise for the simple case will be limited to 6 layers of foil as this suffices for protection in this situation.

What's good to know is the stalkers will spend astronomical sums to make up for vulnerabilities, compared to a TI who spends very little to obstruct the same equipment, good news that is immediately rendered nugatory by the realization the amounts at the disposal of these gangs makes expense a non issue for them.

History

England was at the forefront of radar research in the years leading up to the Second World War. This research led to the very first early warning radar system called "Chain Home". They would later install this system in the first radar stations built around the British Isles and other locations in America, the purpose of which was early detection of aerial threats.

Personnel at these radar stations noticed that insects, birds and other animals tended to avoid the parts of the installations where the energized antennas were mounted. At times, these creatures would be found dying or dead when it was clear they had not made direct contact with energized circuitry. Reports made of these occurrences aroused great interest in military circles because it pointed to the potential for a new class of radar frequency and microwave weapon. Soon after this, an international arms race based on these weapons would be underway.

Since then, a number of reports have surfaced that point to the fact governments have not flinched to use the technology on their own citizens for purposes of research and control.

It is still not established whether Russian actions were a reaction to, or retaliation for similar activities by American intelligence against Russian civilians or intelligence officers in America or elsewhere, but as far back as 1960, they are known to have launched covert attacks on unsuspecting American Embassy personnel in Moscow. The embassy was bombarded with radar like microwave beams, using the personnel as guinea pigs in low-level electro-magnetic radiation experiments. Three consecutive U.S. ambassadors would lose their lives as a direct consequence of this.

As far as is known, the objective of the Russian experiment was to induce a few of the effects known at the time, of which malaise, irritability and extreme fatigue are some. They falsely believed that the effects would be temporary. It is now known that, depending on the level of exposure, effects of electromagnetic wave exposure can be hard to reverse, and in some instances are permanent. These effects have thus far been expanded to include cataracts, blood changes that induce heart attacks, malignancies, circulatory problems and permanent deterioration of the nervous system. It is also not a given that effects appear immediately after exposure. They can sometimes take a decade or so to become evident.

The British army is also known to have used the conflict in Northern Ireland as a testing ground for these new technologies, specifically aimed at refining methods of controlling large populations. They built watchtowers over underground, three- story bunkers filled with computers that used sonar and infrared technology to not only watch people through the walls of their homes, but thwart the IRA by removing the cover they would otherwise have had, and also by launching through-the-wall attacks on those they considered strategic targets. This fact was brought to light by the sudden rise in the number of conditions or deaths related to radiation attacks, or when British soldiers would reveal they were seeing more than is humanly possible by taunting local residents, especially Irish women, with detailed descriptions of the underwear they were wearing on that particular day.

According to a claim made by Walter Bowart, the American author of "Operation Mind Control", one group of British females demonstrating against American nuclear weapons or waste in Britain were attacked with a microwave weapon in 1989. His claim was given credibility not only because it was already known America had engaged in directed energy attacks or abuse of unwitting civilians, such as mind control experiments carried out by the notorious psychiatrist Ewen Cameron on Canadians in Montreal, funded by the CIA, but also due to symptoms presented by the demonstrating females that pointed to microwave exposure. These included anomalies with menstrual cycles, spontaneous abortion, other (unspecified) feminine problems, retinal burning, inner ear problems and rapidly growing tumors.

How DEW's Work

There are two main frequencies used in most covert DEW attacks. They are the Extremely Low Frequency (ELF) waves, and the Extremely High Frequency (EHF) waves.

ELF is a radio frequency from 3 to 30 hertz, which is in the same range as the human brain's electrical activity frequency of 14 hertz. This likeness in range makes it possible to use the frequencies to interfere with, overload and jam, or tune into the electrical patterns in specific areas of the brain. They can as such be used to induce illness, negative mental inclinations, cause paralysis by overloading the brain's own signals in the same manner militaries jam enemy communications by sending stronger signals at the same frequency, or even tune into the nervous system to interpret thought, create visual or vocal evocations.
Specific frequency effects required for "operational use", meaning application in real life situations, especially warfare, have already been identified through extensive research and experimentation on both animals and humans. This means it is already known which frequency to apply to gain a precise reaction within targeted areas of the human brain.

As the name suggests, EHF are high frequency radio bands, running the range of frequencies from 30 to 300 gigahertz. These frequencies have a wavelength of one to ten millimeters, giving it the name millimeter band or millimeter wave. They are commonly used in radar sets and microwave ovens. The principal advantage of EHF over ELF lies in the fact that transmissions are made along strait lines, making it possible to beam them accurately into small areas, unlike ELF that tends to scatter widely.

EHF, or microwaves, are generated by a device called a "Magnetron" in which electrons, generated by the heated cathode, are moved by the combined force of a magnetic and electrical field. The cathode is a hollow cylinder with the outside coated with barium and strontium oxide electron emitters. A large cylindrical anode containing a large number of resonant cavities, normally of quarter- wavelength, on the inner surface, is arranged concentrically around the outside of the cathode. The complete assembly is sealed inside a vacuum enclosure.

When switched on, the magnetron generates an electrical field in a radial manner between anode and cathode, while the magnetic field is coaxial with the cathode. The maximum power output is naturally limited by the size of the individual Magnetron but research indicates the largest can generate a stream of microwave pulses at up to ten million watts per pulse. The resulting beam can be focused in much the same way as a camera lens, from ultra wide angle to telephoto, creating area or pinpoint capability.

Obstruction

Due to the obvious advantages of EHF over ELF, microwaves are the beam of choice in covert warfare. They are also the most lethal especially due to the inside out manner they affect targets. Making the obstruction of these waves a priority, and then moving on to manage the other waves, for example neutralizing the effects of ELF that are mostly used in mind control, is the mainstay of the simple method. This means you do not have to apply all the obstructions listed here to be safe. It will be sufficient if you put 6 layers of foil on your wall, take the precautions concerning mind control frequencies, and take the advice given on health. These three measures combined are not beyond the means of the average citizen, and will be enough to ensure you remain of resilient health.

At low to medium power settings, a microwave beam can be stopped in the same way as a layer of cooking foil placed over food in a microwave oven, reflecting the waves back and preventing the food from cooking.

The standard number of kitchen foil layers that will suffice to block out the higher power settings is 6. These should be placed on a wall or floor where attacks are known to emanate from, or all if there is no certainty. The layers can be pasted onto the wall, ensuring that the paste is placed on the wall instead of the foil, and that subsequent layers are only applied when the paste has hardened. They can also be taped to the wall from end to end, ensuring that they overlap where they meet so as to avoid the creation of gaps through which beams can slip through. When taping the foil, make sure the foils are layered flat to avoid the possibility of reflection, which could lead some waves into the interior. Remember always that foil conducts electricity, and should never be tucked below plug or switch covers.

Various kinds of foil wallpaper are also available at retail outlets, which can also be used for the purpose. These wallpapers come with a single metal layer, or metalized plastic film on a paper backing, in as many textures and colors as ordinary wallpaper, making them suitable for any interior.

The disadvantage of foil wall paper is that it provides a single layer of protection that becomes insufficient as soon as the power setting of the magnetron is increased.

Sheet metal can also be used instead of the above materials. It provides much more protection, with one layer sufficing for all levels of protection. Ensure that the layers overlap by at least 5 centimeters, and that the layers are laid out flat against each other throughout. This minimizes room for leakage. Cover holes made by nails and such with layers of foil, or wrap the foil around nails right down to the metal to dissipate any waves that could filter through. Stalkers are known to scan for the smallest of spaces in the TI's defense.

Metalized paint is also available at hardware stores. It can be painted over walls, windows and doors. Layers of paint are necessary for increased protection. The paint can be insulated and left as is, and will provide some degree of protection.

This kind of protection can be stepped up by energizing the metal paint with a phase and frequency alternating current. This will create a primitive "faraday cage" that jams out most transverse EMF waves, the energy waves used for through-the-wall spying and other attacks. It is recommended that you hire an electrician to help you with this.

Soundproofing foam also has the capacity to jam out some sound waves that are used in DEW attacks, examples being ultrasound and scalar neutrino waves, which are also transverse. To the list of waves that are used for spying can be added the sub-nuclear energy waves, that can effectively be jammed with sheets of lead similar to those used in lead coffins, layered with other metals and plastics, of which copper, zinc and vinyl are some.

Relaxing while playing music is a good way of neutralizing the effects that mind control waves have on the mind. These waves can also lock onto metals and plastics in or on the body. You can decrease this conductivity by taking metal cleansers such as coriander herbs, and acidic vitamins, and removing metallic cavities. A vinegar bath can clean the skin pores of tiny nanotech metals and plastics.

In instances of partial obstruction, especially when the location the beams are coming from is known, it is important to check the access angles carefully, so that protection isn't limited to the house's interior design. For example, if the suspect location is in a diagonal location, then it makes sense to cover the entire wall with whatever you use for obstruction on that side, including the floor, rather than just the wall, as beams from that direction are bound to pass through part of the wall and floor. If it is the reverse, then the roof and the wall should both be covered.

The ideal rooms in the house to place obstructions are those where the most time is spent, for example the study, living room and bedroom. Research carried out on a large group of women who had been exposed to a leaking microwave oven, in an open plan office over a period of many months, revealed that the degree of damage in each case was directly proportional to the distance from the leaking microwave oven. It is as such important that areas in the house where most time is spent, for example the sofa or bed, are placed furthest away from the source of the beam.

A microwave detector, a device that detects microwave leaks, is a must have item in a target's home. It will alert of instances of actual attack, taking away a lot of the stress related to being in a situation where one does not know the exact moment they are exposed to harmful beams. It will also tell the TI whether current measures against DEW are working, so that they can increase the level of protection if need be.

Standard detectors are very sensitive, capable of picking up microwave output as low as one milliwatt per square centimeter.

When a shield is placed less than half way the wavelength of the energy beam from the source, there is what is called "zero node" at the point the wave meets the shield. This makes the metal invisible to the electromagnetic beam, and it will pass through into the interior and onto the target with original intensity.

If a perp has direct access to a shield, all he/she needs to do is find the distance where the zero node circumstance can be created.

Double shields placed at an inaccessible distance in the interior, especially when they are electrified; tackle this vulnerability with distance, and by increasing the shielding potential of the metal. Zero node cannot be achieved if the spacing between the shields is just more than half the wavelength of the energy beam, because then it will be impossible for the beam to be a distance away from either shield that is less than half the wavelength.

Knowing the wavelength involved in DEW attacks is a prerequisite to making this work. Obviously, only the perp will be aware of such technical details. The best a TI can do in the situation is meet the perp on equal terms where that which is not technical is concerned.

Just as the perp searches the target's shield to find holes in the defense through which to launch attacks, moves the DEW further or closer to effect zero node, or searches for other vulnerabilities in the TI's defenses; constant tinkering and upgrading of defenses helps not only offset any advantage the perp may be enjoying in the moment, but also fosters understanding of how the whole thing works, especially by revealing what works better and what is worse.

For example, a single shield of metal on an external wall is useless when zero node can easily be achieved, but erecting a second, adjustable layer on the inside of the protected space helps resolve this problem. The layer will require constant adjustment and thickening from time to time according to perceived incursions.

Microwaves can get through metal if the plasma frequency in the metal is lower than the frequency of the beam. This is what is called "ultraviolet invisibility" of metals. Passing a phase and frequency current through the same metal tremendously decreases this invisibility.

A faraday cage, as indeed any metal shield, is only as good as the thickness of its layers. Increasing the number of layers should be an ongoing process where relief gained from former increases is short-lived, as perps will always attempt to increase power or change frequency to overcome the better obstruction. The entire shield should be so constructed as to easily be upgraded without having to undo previous effort.

Shields in rooms where you will get visitors to whom the obstructions cannot be revealed need to be constructed in such a manner that the finish looks presentable but can easily be changed without much effort or extra expense.

In my experience, the method that worked best at stopping the worst effects of DEW bombardment, at once doing away with ultraviolet invisibility and the creation of zero node, is the double shield made up of 2 X 6 layers of aluminium, insulated from each other with plastic or any other dielectric, then electrified in series. Because the metal has a current running through it, it has less ultraviolet invisibility therefore less material is needed for effective shielding.

Further updates to this structure need only be electrical. A new layer of foils, insulated from the other two, with an independent current running through it, can also be added as need be. In the remote case a method of bypassing this shield is found and new layers cannot be put up quickly enough, there is always the possibility of creating a temporary, smaller shield around the area where most time is spent, for example the sofa or bed, until the work on the wall shield is completed. This smaller shield can also be made up of two layers that are insulated with a dielectric then electrified.

Through the wall spying capabilities are the single most enabling aspect of attacks. It is impossible to know exactly where a target is in a house next door, let alone target specific body parts without this technology. It is also very difficult for a TI who knows something about electricity to launch reprisal attacks using a converted microwave that can be anywhere near successful without the use of this technology. Disabling the ability of the perp to see through the wall is half the battle in dealing with the DEW problem.

Because the perps around me were near enough to be heard, I could always tell what they were reacting to when they rushed across the boards above my flat. I learnt that using through the wall spying technology is not a straightforward activity, especially when I introduced electricity to my shields. Whenever I changed the current running through the shield or reversed the flow of electricity, the perp upstairs would make what always sounded like a panicked reaction. Sometimes there was the sound of confused steps running up and down for a while after that, that would suddenly die down, indicating some kind of solution had been found.

This sequence of events would be played out almost every time I made any electrical changes to the shields, leading me to conclude there was an urgent requirement to adjust the equipment in order to be able to see again.

Obviously, installing a device that keeps changing the flow of electricity, increasing and decreasing the wavelength and voltage at random, would make it almost impossible for the perp to view the TI in their house, unless the perp is relying on heat sensitive technology. This however has the vulnerability of not being able to detect beyond thermal materials.

Making a double shield is easy and does not take a lot of time. I will pass you through some basics here. Get an electrician to do it for you if you are not familiar with how electricity works, otherwise observe health and safety procedures.

Wear rubber gloves while you work. Wear rubber shoes to prevent the flow of electricity through your body to the ground. Always insulate naked wires and other conducting materials before connecting to the mains.

Use this method only when you are sure no pets will claw, or children scratch away at the insulation and get electrocuted. Do not lay the foil wallpaper or kitchen foil under electricity sockets, unless you know the construction and purpose of each part. Do not let any part of your shield come in contact with central heating or other metal plumbing.

Perps will try to attack you more when they know you are attempting to build a defense against DEW's. I have endured the worst attacks just at the time I was constructing a shield at my flat, so severe they left me numb in vital areas for days after that. In a way, the perp is afraid they will lose control, and try to make up for what they will not be able to do to you at once. They also know the effect of the beams on your system. Attacking you at the moment you are trying to help yourself makes you do a shoddy job of it.

It is therefore of paramount importance that you protect yourself as much as possible before beginning. Make a hat from at least 6 layers of foil and roll about the same number around your torso and genital area. You can use other kinds of sheet metal for the purpose. Do not be discouraged from doing this even when an insane image of a medieval knight stares at you in the mirror. It will decrease the amount of damage that can be done to your body and ensure you do the job properly.

There are a lot of flexible shielding materials that can be purchased from retail outlets that will also serve the purpose. Some of these materials can be Googled and ordered online. They are supple enough to be worn but be aware they are designed for protection against lower intensities of electromagnetic radiation, for example mast emissions. You may need to layer them up just as you would the foil to get better defense.

You may also need to play your favourite music while you work to cancel out the effects of mind control frequencies launched at you in a bid to discourage you from working.

The shield in question can also be constructed using any kind of sheet metal, given it is a high conductivity material. Ensure that the layers overlap by at least a few centimetres, and that they are laid flat against each other without gaps through which the radiation could penetrate.

You will need sufficient conductive material, in this case kitchen foil that can be purchased for as little as £2 for a 30 meter roll at Morrison's, wallpaper paste, insulation foam or a dielectric like plastic, a few meters of electric wire, an electrical appliance, preferably a bedside lamp, duct tape and a current testing device.

Paste six layers of wallpaper onto the wall, ensuring you paste the wall first. Do not paste, but tape the plastic or other dielectric to the finished layers, or smear the insulation foam and wait until it is dry. Seal the edges of the plastic where there is overlapping to prevent the paste fluids seeping through and causing a short circuit.

Alternately, you can paste the plastic onto the wall, but you should seal the overlapping edges and consider the long waiting time till the paste dries.

Paste the rest of the foil until you have six or more layers up then insulate the last layer as well. Make sure you leave exposed foil for both the inner and outer layer to attach you electricity wire to.

If you are having trouble pasting the foil, then you can simply tape it neatly to the wall, ensuring each one is rolled out then taped in place, the next rolled out overlapping the former by at least a centimetre. Tape individual parts together from end to end. Repeat this process if you are using the dielectric.

After checking whether the colors are connected properly, remove the insulation from part of the electric cable of the lamp, then cut the negative wire. Connect the wire leading to the plug to the inside of the shield, and the other to the outside (see illustration below). Insulate the electric wires and plug the appliance into the wall.

The lamp will not go on, but the current tester will indicate a live current on the exterior of the wall.

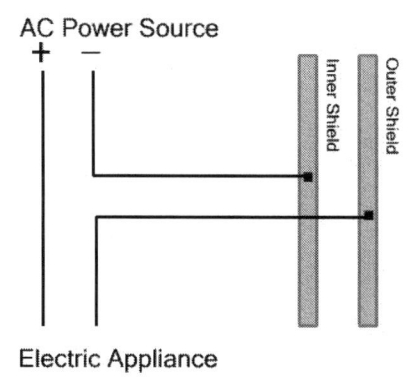

AC Power Source

Inner Shield Outer Shield

Electric Appliance

This shield will work very well against most electromagnetic beams. It is the structure I have to thank for the fact I have preserved my mind and body.

If you experience unbearable attacks while working on this shield and are discouraged from continuing, or it takes too long as a result, then try to do a single layer of foil for each instead, following the instructions given before. This shield works well even with a single layer of foil on each side. You will later be able to complete the process by increasing the number of layers on the accessible, inside shield, after which you can put up a layer of insulation and another 6 layers of foil.

Alternatively, you can electrify a single layer of foil or sheet metal. This will increase the shielding capacity of the metal tremendously, but is still not the better option. There are more RF that can be jammed out with two or more layers than with just one.

If electrifying is not the thing for you, then you can simply earth the faraday cage. If caught by surprise by DEW at a time you cannot work on your defenses, then try earthing your own body to the same point as the faraday cage. Put some oil on a finger, ankle or toe to increase conductivity, tie an electric wire to a ring and slip it on. Your own skin will now act as a shield against radiation.

I have tried this method and, believe me, it made a big difference. The only draw back is, because the skin gets the brunt of the attack, it gets visibly damaged. Facial skin is the most affected, something that would discourage many from using the method, but then I would argue it is better that the skin gets damaged than the major organs. Better to preserve the core upon which the systems will rely for regeneration. As already intimated, this option should be a temporary measure done at times when nothing else is possible.

There is no danger to using this method as, since we are designed to walk the earth barefoot, our bodies are no strangers to the naturally occurring electricity that flows below and on the surface of the earth. In fact, this electricity flowing through the human body may be beneficial if it helps deflect some naturally occurring electromagnetism to the earth. In this case, carpeted housing and foam beds may not be such a healthy thing after all.

Chapter 9
Securing external property

The personal belongings you use, and sometimes have to leave outside your home are not exempt from covert attacks. This means your car, your motorcycle or bicycle, your tractor if you are a farmer, anything that you use for prolonged periods during the day, the interior of which you are exposed to by breathing or touching, can be tampered with in the same manner as the interior of your house. Depending on the rate and lengths of exposure, such property deserves the same security consideration as everything else discussed thus far.

Doorknobs of your car can be smeared with chemical or biological agents that can be absorbed into your body, either through the skin or through the digestive tract by way of hand contact with your mouth, while the interior can be contaminated with the same substances or others that you breath in, entering the body through the lungs. A bike's handlebars or seat can also be smeared with similar harmful substances that can be absorbed into the body through the thinner skin on the back.

If you are involved in public transportation as a bus driver or taxi driver and are not responsible for overnight security of the vehicle, you should take the same measures as you would with your own personal property. There are many ways stalkers can figure out the vehicle you are going to use the next day.

If it is impossible to completely secure personal property you leave outside or avoid getting hit in public places where you are vulnerable to attacks; if you cannot keep your bike indoors, or do not have a garage; cannot keep your bike or car watched when you leave it parked on the streets, cannot keep watching your back when working at the helm of a car, then the best you can do is take measures that both prevent your body being exposed to harmful substances and help maintain mental and physical strength. For example, in cases of personal property, it is a good idea to use gloves before handling doorknobs or handle bars, to wash hands thoroughly in cases of direct exposure. The thickness of the skin on the palm of your hand may hinder absorption of harmful substances into your body, but then you may later wipe your face or handle food, which could have dire consequences. You can also start wearing washable hats as they can protect you from agents fine sprayed onto the back of your head.

If you cannot take your bike indoors at night, then leave it as close to your window as you can, otherwise make sure it is covered. If you cannot keep it watched during the day, then cover the seat when you use it. Any nonporous cover that's comfortable to sit on, that you can carry with you is enough. If you need to use bare hands on some parts, especially when carrying out repairs, ensure you wash the exterior of these parts first before proceeding.

Keep the inside of your car clean. Thoroughly vacuum clean mats, and soap other surfaces. Regular and thorough washing of the car's exterior helps remove dangerous substances that may have been sprayed by passers by, especially those that could lodge inside air shafts. Use warm to hot water as this will help drain away oily substances that are often used in such attacks.

I discovered that the bloating symptoms I displayed after some time in my vehicle disappeared after washing it. Later on, I noticed that relief given by hand washing was never comparable to putting the car through the automated car-wash machine. This may be due to the fact larger quantities of water are poured through the body of the car than is possible with hand washing, even when you use a hose for the purpose, ensuring that more of the harmful substances are washed off.

Avoid using the air inlets that open at the front, sides or back of the car for ventilation. They are the favorite locations for contamination as this draws the harmful fumes into the depths of the car. Keep the shafts on your dashboard shut, and use only the windows for fresh air.

Install a good alarm system in your car to prevent easy access to the interior. At night, always ensure that you park your car in a well lit area, especially one where you or another neighbor can easily keep watch. Placing your car under an automatic light that warns when an intruder nears is a plus. If you have a cover for your car then it is worthwhile to cover the car every time you leave it parked outside. It may be tedious and a bit weird if you are the only one doing this in your neighborhood, but, as already said, it is worth the trouble. It may not offer complete security but it makes the job of accessing the crucial parts difficult. What you want to be doing every step of the way is making it that much harder for the stalkers to reach you.

Chapter 10
Safety While Out and About

In This Chapter
- Staying Alert When You Mingle
- Securing Your Shopping
- Living Rough or Going on the Run

Don't be fooled into believing the information out there that attempts to limit the phenomenon of covert warfare to some locations. It is true that a TI is much more vulnerable in his home, and that most attacks are designed around, and concentrated on this location. There are however circumstances that can make the outdoors preferred over the indoors.

If, for some reason, while you are in your home, your stalkers cannot inflict the kind of damage a day out walking would not be able to clear, or they cannot get to you at all because you are always surrounded by people or have enough security installed, then the next obvious location where attacks can occur is when you are out and about.

Staying Alert When You Mingle

There are all manner of reasons why stalkers follow a target in public. They may want to gain knowledge concerning the effects of an attack launched previously; to see how the skin looks, whether there are some giveaway symptoms, how the TI smells, etc. Sometimes they could merely be checking whether an activity a TI was engaged in previously, for example fitness, has had an effect on their general state. If there has been a positive change, then such observations are recorded for future use. Subsequent stalking activities will involve preventing the target from engaging in the particular activity. I know from experience that these records are also passed on to stalkers in other cities or countries where the TI may move to so that the new stalkers do not need to learn the target's habits, weaknesses and strengths from scratch.

Stalkers may engage in round the clock surveillance to intimidate or inconvenience the victim in a continual war of attrition, or harass for the purpose of repression. Other times they could undertake the activity for the purpose of testing the strength of the personality of the victim, to see what's left after the attacks, or the habits of the victim so they can know their exploitable weaknesses and vulnerabilities.

This last is actually concomitant to all activities, allowing the stalkers to adjust their attack strategy or intensity according to the observations they make. Every action stalkers take against a target is based on the information they have gathered about them and their surroundings, without which mistakes can be made with the potential to expose the stalking, or hamper the elimination process.

For example, if they are not sure the individual being stalked has the potential to reveal their activities, if this revelation is possible through a specific contact, then the initial task will be to sever the link.

Round the clock surveillance provides stalkers with the means by which they can affect the individual's isolation by enabling virtual entry into every facet of the individual's life. It provides the entry point into the target's personality, allowing the person coordinating the activity to know when and which buttons he can safely push. Obsessing with the target is as such a necessary part of any stalking activity. It may look like madness to those not involved, but the stalkers know exactly what they are doing, every step of the way.

Foiling a successful attempt to disrupt one's life, to get isolated, requires foiling the stalker's ability to learn all there is to know about one. This requires meeting the stalkers on their own devious terms.

A target should concentrate on doing those things that annul the advantage of technological resources and numbers that stalkers have, especially their capacity to see through walls, and communicate a target's movements to other people in the direction he/she is heading. This means working at not being obvious, not being predictable, leading stalkers on, rather than sticking to routine, in which case the stalkers will be a step ahead all the time. A TI should concentrate on especially learning to discern situations when they are vulnerable, to learn as much about these situations as will allow them to either avoid, or control events to a degree, if not possess the capacity to turn the tables on the stalkers.

When you go about such deviousness, always differentiate between activities that aid the stalking and alienation process, and those that increase your freedom. For example, if you give chase when you identify a stalker, you are doing something that is not beneficial to you. If you lean out of your window and hurl obscenities and threats at the stalkers down below who are calling out to you, you are going out of your way and doing their job for them. You are reacting to stalker prompting and as such doing exactly what they want you to do; wasting your time.

Let them respond to your activity. This may sound like stating the obvious, since this is what they are doing all the time, but there is a subtle difference here, which is that you ensure this rule is adhered to by making it imperative that though they are watching you wherever you are, they still have to guess what you are going to do next, rather than that they predict everything you will do on account of the study they have meticulously undertaken of your habits enabling them to hinder, frustrate or attack you.

For example, you may be dependent on your car for transportation, but if you come out of your house and find it has been deliberately blocked so you cannot move it, do not even work up a rage. Don't go knocking on everybody's front door asking whose car it is. Leave your car standing there and use public transportation for that day. Develop the kind of flexibility that allows you to be comfortable with any change of method or manner you get around or do things. This defeats their every attempt at psychological harassment, to frustrate, even attack you physically. It makes whatever they do against you seem futile, forcing them to bring the issue out into the open where it can be dealt with on equal terms.

You could be using public transportation to get around, in which case you either use it casually, or at set times every day, going up or down, to and from work, for example. You could also be using your car in the same manner described above. You may be in the habit of regularly eating out or buying meals from a particular, or various takeaway outlets, or may be going out to the same pub every so often. You may be in the habit of going out every weekend, spending the night in various locations, or the one particular place. You might have a favorite location at which you do your shopping every week, or a gym to which you go to work out twice a week.

These habits can be studied in detail, enabling any interested party to be a step ahead of you wherever you go, and in the case of stalkers then they could be capable of preparing an attack at any of the locations you frequent, or preventing you from undertaking any activity that could hamper their operation.

The bus you use at a particular time of day can be anticipated, then boarded by your stalkers, before or after you board. The situation will be assessed and the go ahead for the attack will be given when the coast is clear. They could lay an ambush along the usual route you take to work in your car, forcing you into an accident, if need be. Stalkers could infiltrate or recruit a member of staff at the restaurant you frequent every other day, making possible the task of poisoning you through the food you order. They could find out the kind of woman or man you prefer, and set up a relationship for you, in which case they may get right into your own home as much and as long as they can. A stalker could pose as a friendly fellow at the pub you frequent, waiting for the moment your eye is turned to slip or spray something into your drink.

Once, while standing in a very busy disco, I caught a man red handed as he was about to spray some substance into my beer, when he thought all attention had been diverted. I had put my beer on the counter and turned to observe the figures on the dance floor when I sensed movement behind me, turning around sharply in response. What surprised me about the incident was the man appeared to be a cross between a normal individual, and a spoon face, not really the type you would expect to engage in such an activity.

Stalkers are known to manipulate a victim into corners they know are convenient for attacks, by for example crowding out the places where the TI would usually sit or stand, so that he/she is forced into the location where attacks can easily and covertly be carried out, especially corners where other stalkers are sitting or standing, so that the TI is conveniently surrounded. This tactic of manipulation is carried out throughout the stalking process, wherever the TI may be, with the end objective being to manipulate the victim into absolute isolation where it is easier to eliminate them without causing suspicion.
When launching an actual attack in a public location, a single stalker may suffice, usually launching the attack as he/she passes the victim or the victim's property, including drinks or a plate of food. Other times it is

necessary that a whole gang coordinate the attack, some members acting as lookouts, while others distract the target. This is more so in situations with too many unknowns, where the possibility exists that another person could walk into the room, look the wrong way at the wrong time thus catching the stalkers in the act, or that the possibility exists for self contamination. This last is more so in airborne attacks where stalkers have to remain in the same space as the target while the attack is launched.

I have personally witnessed instances where an airborne attack was launched without the stalkers leaving the space. I believe they are either already inoculated against the agents used in such attacks, or are told how long the agents remain in the air, so that they know how long they need to hold their breath before the harmful substances dissipate to harmless concentrations. Not having the same warning or protection, the victim keeps breathing, as such taking in the full force of the attack.

The first time I was attacked and the stalkers remained in the same location was in London. I was sitting on the top deck of a bus, next to a group of white teenagers; not the age nor appearance you could readily associate with such activity. I had been feeling good that day and was planning to go out and have some fun. I was doing the last leg of the day's activities before I went back home to prepare for the night.

I walked onto this bus in the same high spirits that had followed me throughout the day, but noticed that I walked out feeling rather intoxicated, dizzy, and quite down of spirits. I immediately recognized the substance used from the sensation it left in my nose and mouth as the same that had been used against me in other situations, the same that had been used extensively in prison in Holland, the effects of which are a sudden dryness in the mouth, stiff limbs, lack of coordination, sudden sensitivity of the eyes to the external environment leading to watering, numb mental state, leading to instances where I could come to a stand still, then suddenly regain full consciousness and discover I had forgotten why I stopped.

People can, and do regularly pass all kinds of wind in each other's company, but non can have effects that are as intense and as adverse as those felt with this agent, not even for a man who is allergic to some smells.

Due in most probability to the fact my system had gained some resistance to the agent, I managed to think back through to the moment I had boarded the bus, on to the moment I had disembarked, and remembered that right before the sudden sick feeling, what had been a boisterous group of teenagers sitting around me had suddenly gone silent. I then identified the exact moment I had fallen victim to the attack.

As usual, the faint and vague mental state that follows the attack ensured that I did not become aware of the sudden change or deterioration of mental and physical vitality, preventing me from knowing, let alone reacting to the attack in any way. In a sense, this substance knocks you out of your senses without flooring you, making it impossible for you to notice you have been attacked, especially since the mind becomes sluggish, thought unclear and encumbered, right after the attack.

It might seem that there was no way I could have avoided such an attack, but then on that day I was nothing but very predictable. I walked out of my house at the very same time I usually did, took the same bus, going in the very same direction I always did at the time. I may not have been aware of the particular attack method, as such hardly have been able to avoid being affected by the substance. Only avoidance of habit would have prevented the attack.

The group of teenagers was obviously standing a few bus stops away, looking very normal to those around. They were very easily called by mobile phone and told to board the bus I was about to take. There are as many groups of people that can be placed on a given route in this manner without raising suspicion. If I had not taken that particular bus then the chance of another attack would have been minimized since one attack group would have been going the wrong direction already, while the man coordinating the attack, who was most probably watching me from a house in the neighborhood, would have had a no clue of my next move. The next attack would have been haphazardly arranged, the success of which would have depended on luck.

Do everything possible to avoid being an easy target of attacks. If you have to take the bus at a particular time of day, then try to alter your schedule. Try altering boarding times and locations if the last is not possible due to tight schedule or such. This means you do not wait for your bus at the same place, same time every day, but change time and location by for example waiting for the bus earlier than usual one day, moving up or down the same or a different road, as long as the bus there takes you to the same destination, even when you have to change buses along the way.

Use your memory of what's normal in a given location to determine whether a road or bus is too full for the time of day, or is full of the wrong kind of people. Should you observe suspicious behavior on the road then try an alternative route, stop at a filling station for a coffee or such. Switch from driving slowly to driving quickly, or stop completely and wait by the side of the road till you are sure the trouble has gone. Do anything that forces anyone who wants to stick close to you act unnaturally.

Stalkers will usually use advanced technology to know when a target has woken up, when they have had their shower, and when they are ready to walk out the door. They will time their activities to activities they expect of the TI. If the stalkers know when you take the bus every day, they will ensure a few individuals are waiting for you at a location along the way. If one day you do not just run out of your shower, put your clothes on, take some breakfast and leave, but take some time to read the morning paper, unexpectedly walk out of your house then take a different route to the bus stop from the one you always take; deliberately miss the first bus that comes along even if it is your number, the advanced technology the stalkers are using will be compromised. A stalker who should have been waiting for you at a certain location will be forced to wait longer. The one who entered the bus before will be forced to pass through and get off at the next stop, or make a detour, making his activities that much more obvious.

Should the bus you are on be boarded by a lot of suspicious looking characters, then get off and wait for the next bus. You can also put the trip off if possible, especially when there are repeat occurrences of the same kind of crowd or person getting on. You could also attempt to change the direction you are going so that you arrive from a different direction than usual.

Avoid sitting in the same location every time you get in any public place. Avoid sitting in front of people you find suspicious. Stalkers are also known to fine spray harmful substances into the hair of targets, so that you will experience headaches or other discomforts for some time after that. Because the substances involved in such attacks are water soluble, try to wear washable hats when you are out and about. If you sense the onset of a headache or a similar discomfort to your head, rinse your hair down to the scalp with tap water as soon as you have the opportunity. You will be surprised at the sudden relief you could get from as simple an action as this.

If you go to the gym at a fixed time then you are advised to change this routine to one that cannot be predicted. Picking up the bag you always carry to the gym, walking in the direction of the gym but bypassing it for another location unnerves those following and puts their plans for you in disarray. The next time you will walk in that direction they will not take it for granted you are going to the gym and you can confuse them further by doing something else that's out of the ordinary.

In the gym itself, avoid leaving anything that comes in contact with your body in a locker that is not in a secure location. You can walk in with your gym shoes and leave with them, taking your shower in a location you are sure is secure. Wear training gloves when handling weights. This is advised for better grip and avoidance of callus, but it also prevents contact with harmful substances in case someone chooses to attack you that way.

Some, if not most of these activities you need to take may seem abnormal, but then you are in an abnormal situation and should not flinch from taking appropriate measures. As long as you plan things before hand, you will avoid looking abnormal to friends and others.

You may be outnumbered by your stalkers, and they may know where you are at a given time of the day, but even they cannot cope with sudden changes of schedule in a manner that would not entail revealing some form of strange behavior on their part to the public. Not allowing stalkers to disrupt your life should not only entail ignoring them, but also taking measures that make it harder for them to affect changes to your personality through covert attacks, that will ultimately have the same effect.

Securing Your Shopping

When doing your shopping, keep your basket or wagon watched at all times. Stalkers are known to flood into especially the larger supermarkets when they know the target is doing their periodic shopping. Using numbers, they are capable of distracting the attention of the TI long enough to swap products already in the basket. Their close study of the target's favorite products enables them to switch products in the shelves, right before they know the target will pick them up. The point of all this is to switch a product or article of shopping with one that is contaminated.

Don't get into the habit of picking up the same product from the same shelf all the time. Never pick up a product if it the last one left. Avoid making your shopping from the same shop every time. Avoid especially doing the shopping on the exact same day of the week or month, at the exact same time, in the exact same shop.

Avoid depending on big supermarkets for your purchases as they tend to be the favorite locations for such attacks because of their impersonal nature. Smaller shops have a limited number of customers whom the shop owner mostly knows. These shops are also much tighter with security so that suspicious behavior of the kind described here is almost impossible.

Vary your shopping, and shorten the number of days before refreshing your supplies. This not only prevents predictability of shopping activity itself, but also updates your home supplies so that duration of exposure to contamination is reduced in cases where your security is compromised.

Going on the Run

There are manners that a person will be attacked that allow for the possibility of flight, once the attacks are recognized for what they are, and financial or physical states of the victim at the moment of attack, or recognition of attack, that also enable escape.

Unfortunately, attacks described in this book are seldom meant to be survived, mentally or otherwise. Whistleblowers, conscientious objectors or activists are not necessarily misfits in any society. Driving them out of the community on this basis cannot as such be the objective of the attack. In most of these cases, forcing flight is the professed reason, the stalker rallying tool. For those pulling the strings, the flight of their target usually only displaces the problem, making it possible for the individual to evade elimination and continue with the very same threatening activities in a different location, living to fight another day, as it were. For this reason, the capacity to flee is almost always denied the victim.

Since stalkers are not told the truth about the matter, it will not be rare that they will intimate the wrong reason for the harassment to the victim. It is also possible that the people behind the stalking instruct the stalkers to let the target know this is why they are being attacked, only in order to distract the victim.

What should be remembered is stalkers are not privy to the number of combined attacks the target is having, because individuals within the gang of stalkers contribute attacks at different moments, nor do they know the methods being employed by other stalkers. They do not know what the person coordinating the attacks knows, which could be that the combined attacks leave the victim incapable of much action, least of all running out of the city or country.

This is not to say you should never flee from the city or country where you are experiencing covert attacks. The best advice for victims of covert warfare is to leave the area where attacks are occurring, as soon as they can. However, care should be taken with the choice of destination. Organized citizen stalkers usually operate on a national level, so that moving from city to city will not end the problem. Most of these structures are international, so that moving from one country to another, especially to one that has similar interests regarding the issue, is futile. The stalking will simply be taken over by the new authority, the recorded information on the target will simply be handed over so that full scale stalking can commence immediately.

Though it remains true that there are some things a person can do in one country that they cannot do in another, there are behind the scenes relationships that determine how governments react to certain situations that are not in keeping with these realities. The differences that most people observe between countries, especially the various freedoms enjoyed by various nationalities, do not say anything about what is really tolerated or not. There are pacts, relationships, agreements, interests, conventions, secret governments, international structures, secret societies, methods of oppression, etc. governing the behavior of individual governments that the majority of citizens are not aware of. Some activities may look tolerated in some countries only because cases of people crossing the line are dealt with surreptitiously, whereas in other countries they are openly punished. If a hidden but powerful body in one country makes it impossible for an individual to live or conduct certain activities there, chances are that the government of the country where the individual runs to will be put under some kind of pressure to mete out similar treatment, if not that this government is run by the same body and will do the same without prompting, albeit using methods that are different from the former.

This is the reason it is imperative that you provide yourself with as much pertinent information on policy of especially the country you want to flee to as will prevent getting into the same problem all over again. If you know why you are under attack, then check the record of treatment of similar cases by the government in the country of interest. Avoid relying for such information on common impressions, especially since these could be based on falsehoods generated by the ideals of people to whose imagination such a world might be beyond. You could also find out what your survival chances are where you intend to go, whether you can help yourself out of a similar situation; whether you can earn a descent living or will end up on the streets.

Keep in mind that it is almost impossible to get into a situation you cannot get out of in a place you know, whereas you will have to learn how to do the same things in an unfamiliar culture, so that getting out of similar situations may be much harder.

Chapter 11

Mental and Physical Health

In This Chapter
- Health Check and Medication
- Meditation Based Healing
- Physical Exercise
- Healthy Mental Attitude

There are a lot of things you can do to maintain good mental and physical health even when under the most intense of attacks. The point of all efforts is to afford the body the resources it requires to take the force of the attacks, and where damage has been done, the capacity to heal. Your mental state is vital to how you fare in general. Medication is a must in some instances, especially where biological and chemical agents, mind control and DEW attacks are being used, or known to have been used.

Health Check and Medication

If you can trust the health center in your neighborhood, then there are medications available that help against the effects of mind control and other DEW attacks. Take note however that there are very few countries that have passed legislation against electronic harassment that makes it a requirement that doctors, lawyers and law enforcement take claims of this nature seriously. Where DEW attacks are acknowledged, your claims are handled according to set down procedure, which could include filing of the claim and investigation.

In countries where no laws exist against mind control and other DEW attacks, claims of this nature will usually land you with a mental health specialist, even in a mental institution. The way to work around this is to claim you are suffering from a brain disease that's not considered a mental health problem.

Electronic attacks, especially mind control, can cause seizures and brain dysfunctions. You can therefore claim you are having seizures as this is not considered a mental disease, and most medications against this condition will also work against the effects of electronic harassment. Tegretrol is a seizure medication known to work well against the effects of electronic harassment.

There are a lot of health products available at chemists and some natural remedy shops where especially medication that is good for the brain can be bought. Consult a medical specialist on their use if necessary, and always ensure you read the directives of use.

In cases where poisons are used in an attack, determine what the particular agent is, or the group it belongs to by the symptoms, otherwise have a professional do this for you Get treatment for the condition, otherwise administer the medication yourself where possible.

Arsenic is one poison that is commonly used in attacks because of its general availability. Symptoms of arsenic poisoning start with headaches, confusion and drowsiness. As the poisoning progresses, convulsions and changes in fingernail pigmentation may occur. In acute stages of exposure, symptoms may include diarrhea, vomiting, blood in the urine, cramping muscles, hair loss, stomach pain, and more convulsions. The organs of the body that are usually affected by arsenic poisoning are the lungs, skin, kidneys, and liver. If not treated, coma or death will be the result.

If you suspect you are being exposed to arsenic, your diet needs to include lots of sulfur. Sulfur can eliminate some of the arsenic from the body. The foods that contain sulfur are; eggs, onions, beans, legumes, and garlic. Sulfur can also be bought and taken in tablet form. The amino acid that provides sulfur is cysteine.

Chelation therapy is an option you should consider in cases of heavy metal poisoning like arsenic. Chelation therapy is used to remove toxic metals that clog the system such as cadmium, arsenic, lead and mercury from the body. The procedure has been done for some forty years in the United States and is safe. Chelation therapy is a series of injections of ethylenediaminetetra aacetic acid (EDTA) that is done in a doctor's office.

You can also do chelation therapy at home with over the counter chelation formulas bought at a drug store. Most are made with alfalfa, garlic, fiber, turin and selenium. Alfalfa liquid or tablets, taken three times daily with meals, detoxifies the liver and chelates substances from the body. Coenzyme Q(10) improves circulation of the blood which allows the toxic substances to leave the body. L-Lysine, an amino acid, detoxifies harmful heavy metals from our systems. Rutin and apple pectin can be taken to bind with unwanted toxic metals and remove them from the body by way of the intestinal tract.

There are no home made cures I know for biological agents used in covert warfare. Unless you do know of a manner to cure some conditions yourself, the best thing you should do whenever you recognize symptoms of disease is go to a doctor. There are a lot of virulent strains of diseases that could be used in an attack, some of which have no cures, others that can only be cured when identified in the early stages.

Meditation Based Healing

Human beings, as indeed all animals, are electrical. This means we depend on electrical impulses for bodily functions. The brain works on the basis of electronic impulses in the ELF frequencies for thought, moods, memory, and control of limbs and other organs. Exposure to external magnetic and electromagnetic fields affects the electrical equilibrium in the body. This imbalance can cause a wide range of negative physical states and conditions.
Electronic attacks for the purpose of mind control disrupt the natural electronic equilibrium that maintains a balanced personality, and could create negative mental habits, cycles, and feedback loops. Thinking against these instilled negative habits, when they have been identified, helps change the negative feedback loops caused by the electronic attacks, helping to maintain a positive personality. This is useful when you are a target for covert warfare as your need not to be isolated will not be rewarded with negative personalities; meaning you will attract positive people because you are positive yourself.

Meditation is a very good way of bringing balance back to the system. Yoga is one form of meditation developed by ancients and is based on knowledge of the primacy of frequencies to the existence of matter itself. It as such approaches the problem of electronic warfare on its own terms.

Ancients knew the importance of frequency balance within the body, and also knew how to use the body to affect states where the mind was positively influenced. In yoga, the peaceful state of mind that's a prerequisite for entering higher states of consciousness and perception of spiritual reality is but a balancing out of negative energies or frequencies within the body, removing as such the subjective that hinders clear thought.

Yoga incorporates in its method the use of steady breathing as a means of leveling and harmonizing the electrical impulses of the entire physical being. The notion here is that by using natural means, such as conscious control of breathing and other physical movements, a state of harmony of frequencies is achieved that frees the spiritual from the physical confines, heightening the level of consciousness.

This unencumbered level of being, also called the alpha state, allows the consciousness to enter higher levels of being and perception. The after effect is that the body not only conducts more balanced frequencies, but begins to generate them as well. Development of this capacity to generate balanced frequencies has the effect of enabling the physical being to create its own living environment, within which it can prosper, irregardless of external environment.

Physical Exercise

Make it a habit to be as mobile as is possible under the circumstances. A simple walk through the neighborhood every day goes a long way in maintaining a certain level of fitness. Visit the local gym once in a while. Better yet, get a membership at a local gym and start exercising regularly. Start off slowly, with light exercise, then progress on to much more arduous forms of exercise when the body permits.

Physical exercise, especially the arduous kind, is a process that includes damage to the body, especially the muscles, inducing the need to mend them; the progressive lifting of heavier weights and routines that take the body to new heights of endurance. This is equal to the unnatural introduction of an environment that arouses within the body the natural capacity to adapt to new demands, which in this situation means to mend faster and get stronger. The body's natural reaction as such is to cope with the new demands, which when combined with proper nutrition, sufficient rest for recuperation, results in an actual increase of the body's regenerative capacities. It is precisely this capacity that someone under the debilitating attack of covert warfare needs most. The victim then stands a better chance of easily reversing even those effects known to be near permanent in many cases.

Be careful as stalkers will always try to throw a wrench in your program if they can. In most cases, it is essential that you are sure the substances you consume after doing any kind of exercise, which helps in the recuperation process, are free of contaminants. Carry food with you if you are not sure about the security in your home, or simply make it a habit to do the day's shopping after any strenuous activity. This will provide your body with an uncontaminated supply of food when you need it most.

If the stalkers are using DEW and you have not installed defense against these, then take every opportunity to get some fresh air, especially after bouts of strenuous activity. Stay away from the area where attacks occur for as long as is possible. Make it a habit to sleep in different locations, if this is possible. Do anything to minimize the time you are exposed to harm. This gives the body that much more relief from the attacks to maintain a given level of health, enabling fast recuperation and improving the general physical state.

Never train in areas where room exists to contaminate your surroundings, or launch DEW attacks on you.

Always remember that the tenacity with which a TI is followed, from street to street, from home to home, from city to city, and sometimes from country to country, points at desperate hidden figures with the means and also determination to make this possible. The need is such they have to see the attacks sustained through the clock, to the very end.

They will not stop especially when the TI engages in activities beneficial to their well being, for example fitness. Obviously, unless the location you train in is selected carefully, you are not safe from attacks wherever you are, on the street on in some gym.

Avoid jogging in high density residential areas where narrow streets run through houses on both sides. Microwaves can pass through walls, and though the strength decreases with distance, much more so when there is moisture in the air, they can still be very effective at the shorter ranges.

There is almost no place to hide in an environment where pedestrians have to keep to pavements and walk strait lines bypassing parked cars to get where they are going as the distance across even the widest of streets is well within the effective range of a lot of these devices, especially when placed on upper floors of houses at either end of the street.

Considering there are a lot of TI's in any locality, perps situated around them will be used to attack other people passing through the area, as long as the need is there.

This is just logical.

Try as much as possible to jog in areas you are sure cannot be infested with perps. Parks, industrial areas or low density neighbourhoods where houses are spread far apart are good for such recharging of the mind and soul, as the distances the beams have to travel renders them quite ineffective in the end.

Attacks launched at you while out and about are not the worst because complete isolation of individual body parts and organs is difficult, and the attacks can only last a short period since the TI is soon out of range. It is still important to think here of the damage, short and long term, that can be inflicted on a heart beating hard, lungs functioning at maximum capacity, that are at the same time bathed in harmful electromagnetic waves, as you jog along.

If you have to jog in such an environment, then carry a gadget that can warn of attacks. Be aware that living tissue absorbs microwave beams, and ensure that the sensor is not placed away from the suspected or obvious source of attack as no beams will reach it. Take note of radiation hotspots and then map out your jogging route that avoids these hotspots.

Radio Frequency (RF) detectors are best suited to detecting DEW attacks as the most lethal beams are well within the detection range of most. They are however best used in combination with other kinds of detectors, for example ELF sensors, as they come with serious limitations.

Though not as effective at detecting actual microwave bombardment as the former, a gauss meter will warn when high ELF fields are encountered. These emissions are a real health hazard, but they are part of the technologically advanced times we live in. They are all around us and detection does not necessarily suggest perp activity. The device is useful at indicating the proximity of a high power appliance, which most DEW's are. A microwave oven can create ELF fields that can be picked up 10 meters from all angles of the source by a gauss meter at high sensitivity, in contrast to a boiler, TV or electric cooker that makes a meter of noise, if that. They are as such reliable as evidence of attack where an RF meter is left wanting, and no visual identification of an ELF source, for example power lines, can be made.

Select the gym or other enclosed space you train in carefully. Make sure it is a freestanding building and/or does not have homes within effective DEW range, and also check the kind of clientele that frequents the gym before joining in order to know if it is safe and distinguish changes in future. Such places can easily get infested with perps who can launch all manner of contamination attacks designed to prevent you benefiting from the training activity.

Wear gloves to prevent direct contact with surfaces that can be contaminated with dangerous substances in anticipation of your next move, an easy thing to do in a gym environment where training often involves changing machines in turns, or repeated sets at the same machine.
Go into such locations when you can train without looking over your shoulder all the time. Enter when the location is not too busy, or go with trusted friends. Always watch your surroundings without appearing paranoid, ensuring there is no suspicious behaviour. Leave the premises when it becomes apparent you are being set up for the kill.

Go to the showers only when there is no chance of overcrowding. Avoid showers that are in the direct water flow to others.

It is actually advisable to take a shower before and after your training session in the safety of your home, away from locations where it is almost impossible to avoid a hit, even when you keep your eyes wide open. Perps are known to force things when they get desperate, and in situations where they get too obvious, you might just end up with a case on your hands.

Healthy Mental Attitude

How you fare under the circumstances will not only depend on how much you can fend off actual attacks on your mental and physical being, the effects of which have the potential to induce a negative mental state, but on how you manage any mental state that may result, and especially your attitude to people you have to deal with as you go through the ordeal, including your stalkers.

Never for once allow your stalkers to indirectly control what security measure you install apart from those you decide to use in direct response to attacks you know you require to protect yourself from. Keep on the lookout for loopholes, never discarding or discontinuing any of the measures you use whenever you get new ones, but never believe the latest measure has caused the biggest difference.

Stalkers know which measures are working, and which are not. They will try to influence you on some measures you take against attacks, by for example direct reference to a system they want you to think is useless, laughter about a state as you pass them by. They can manipulate attacks to make it seem specific measures are not working. If you respond to such "suggestions", you may take out the good security measures, leaving yourself vulnerable to attacks.

My experience is that when I thought I had found a better replacement, stalkers would give me the impression their attacks were indeed better foiled, whereas in reality they had momentarily stopped a particular attack for the purpose of giving me that very impression, only to launch heavier attacks when I least expected it. There are those cases where this is due to increase in output power of the attack device to bypass increased security, but there are also cases I know where this was not the case. This happened especially in instances where existing measures were sufficient but cumbersome to apply. I only found relief by going back to the measure I replaced.

Stalkers will alter frequencies if those they used before can be blocked by the new obstructions you installed. They will increase the power of the microwave when they find out you have a single layer of foil on your walls, or will change from switching the article of food you buy to offering you poisoned food through a seemingly friendly person. They can take the contamination to the place you believe to be out of bounds of such activities. This includes moving ahead of your appointments, so that they may be able to get to your boyfriend or girlfriend before you go there for dinner, etc. If you are going to be careful with your food, then this means "all food", irregardless you eat the food at your mothers.

The last may sound a bit too much for some, as it has the potential to alienate close ones, but realize there is no area of your life that is out of bounds for attacks. There are no attacks that are beneath or beyond the capabilities of gang members. Attacking innocent civilians is their way of life, after all. Other people can be included into the routine with or without adversely affecting their health, if by this they are only attacked occasionally when you are there, or regularly. You should also remember that stalkers can find out what articles the relative or friend buys for you alone, so that they may be able to run ahead of them and slip a contaminated bottle of red wine, for example; into their basket because they know it is meant for you.

You can take measures against indirect contamination and alienation from friends and relatives by getting involved to some extent in the purchasing activity, if this can be done without raising questions in the mind of the other. Do anything to increase security while at the same time ensuring your actions are not alienating the relative or friend.

Also, keep an eye out for signs your friends or family are being attacked themselves. In cases where you notice symptoms, never bombard them with what you believe is happening to them, but slowly introduce them to the reality. You can allude to the symptoms, for example, and, without connecting it to covert warfare, get them as far as taking a test if you believe this will help. You can provide them with literature that introduces them to the world of covert warfare.

A good friend of mine who came to lodge with me developed the same enlarged pores on the nose and cheeks that had been attracting so much attention to me at my working place. At the time, I was in the habit of telling people I was under attack, and had only succeeded to convince them I was either mentally unstable or sick, or both. I took up the same line of approach with my friend and ended up alienating him. In fact, he avoided me entirely after that. As I would later learn, he had concluded I was misinterpreting symptoms, whereas I knew he had developed the same symptoms as I had in a very short time, this itself proof I was not imagining the whole thing.

I actually pointed out the symptoms he had developed, and used them as proof of the covert warfare I knew I was a victim of, providing him with details of my previous life experiences, specifically the fact I sometimes lived with a mother of two who had not shown any of the symptoms because she never came to my place; that the symptoms disappeared when I slept for prolonged periods at her house, only ending up making him suspect I had infected him. Educating him about the world of covert warfare first, bringing the world that was still beyond his imagination that much closer to his level of understanding would have done everybody involved much more good than harm.

Always ensure that you install full measures. This means that when you want to block out electromagnetic radiation you use wallpaper foil, kitchen foil or sheet metal that will not be penetrated by simply increasing the power level. Use an amount of cover that will suffice even when the stalkers use military grade equipment. The last is an exaggeration, but then I use it as a guide. You should be aware that if it were not for the reality they want victims to die slowly, as such resembling natural causes, stalkers possess the capacity to end your life immediately, whether this is with poisons or DEW. Full measures take this power away from them, so that they will be forced to take self defeating measures.

Resist the temptation to frighten your stalkers off. Never think certain overt actions have the potential to act as deterrents. These groups are way too dedicated to be deterred, under too much pressure to be afraid of especially a single individual. Otherwise the activity makes it that much more of a game for them. The job is one sided enough as it is. They obsess and play games on you without your knowledge, without your participation, in a way playing against their selves. This means their games have meaning to the group alone. You will simply liven up what is otherwise a dull game by calling them to the challenge. Reacting to what they do or deliberately showing them what you are doing to protect yourself spurs them on. Threats and measures become challenges that add thrill to their game, as well as take you further away from your own life.

Never lead stalkers on to the measures you are taking against attacks. Let them discover the hard way what you have installed, or what you have in store for them. Keep a low profile and remain unpredictable when you go snooping for measures against attacks. Advertising will not deter them, but will simply inform of what they should expect. As such, they can easily go out of harm's way.

Violence against a gang member caught in the act should never be considered as this will usually bring revenge attacks. A TI is always surrounded and outnumbered, alone against a united force that is much better trained and equipped. You must always defend yourself when attacked, but never allow them to provoke you to violence against a reverse act that is in itself innocuous. Remember that today's gangs also utilize the same baiting tactics as the Nazi's used against Jews. In cases where you assault a gang member, you will have a number of witnesses testify against you even when you are not in the wrong, so that you, not the one who provoked the violence, will get arrested. Remember that some members of law enforcement are also involved. As long as the attack stays in the innocuous region, for example spitting at you, just remember to keep your dignity.

Do not consider the possibility man to man communication with the attacking group might resolve some issues or think to make deals with them. Avoid any personal interaction with gang members. You do not know who they are, especially not their past. Some of these individuals are guilty of crimes you could not imagine. This in itself makes them unsuitable for any kind of interaction or deal.

Remember that their main objective is to alienate you from your friends and family. Their main objective is to alienate you from your life. Make this difficult. Ignoring their activities as much as possible is a very good way of doing this. Reacting to the group in any way is like taking your hands off the wheel of your life while on the road, which amounts to doing their job for them. Some people have noticed that ignoring the activities of these gangs actually stopped the attacks. It is not guaranteed however that this will work in your case too, but it is worth a try.

You should beware and resist attempts at conditioning. In trying to alienate you from society at large, gang members will try to associate certain members of society with gang activity, so that eventually you will suspect stalking activity when you come across a similar situation. A stalker dressed in a suit will for example look up from a newspaper and make gestures that make you realize he is one of your stalkers. This scene will be repeated in different places, as much as possible, so that you will suspect the next man you find wearing a suite and reading a newspaper to be a stalker, even before he has looked up from the newspaper, let alone at you.

Stalking always involves manipulation. It can be identified as aggressive, but other times it can be harmless. Being a target of covert warfare is not usually knowing what will happen next, wondering when they will finally kill you.

Breaks in life, especially when you need them most, can come from the very same people attacking you. The effect on your psyche can be negative in the sense you will start feeling those who are attacking you are actually magnanimous, especially when you realize the ease with which they could have ended it all for you. You may start to believe they spared your life, and as such start siding with a projected point of view, at which stage you definitely will get the Stockholm Syndrome. Always remember who put you in whatever straits you get into to maintain a realistic perspective on the situation. Putting you in a tight spot then saving you from it is manipulation, not magnanimity.

Always expect people who lend you a hand, give you employment, etc. to become targets of covert attacks. Do not let this affect the rate at which you associate with people. This is doing the stalkers' job for them. You are a gregarious being who needs others to survive, especially when you are in such a situation. Accepting to stay alone is tantamount to committing suicide. As usual, do not directly reference such activity to anyone you suspect is under attack, but keep a habit of educating everyone you come close to of the phenomenon, especially of ways to know when they are under attack, or someone else is under attack.

Never show fear as this makes individual members bolder in attacks against you. Not being fearful means not showing a reaction when they follow you, for example, or when they corner you. Avoid getting cornered as this is the last thing you want to happen when you are under the situation, but should it happen then the last thing you want to do is show fear, as this will work against you.

Senior citizens or other infirm individuals are used in stalking activities, but they remain aware of their physical abilities compared to the TI's. If an old man threatens a younger, much more physically able man, he is usually hiding his fear, but when he smells fear, then the gate is opened for more abuse from the same individual. Remain as calm and relaxed as you can manage to be under any circumstance that may arise. This is the best way of concealing fear.

If you can afford it, then hire a private detective. This may be useful when the source of the attacks is an individual, but is almost useless against attacks initiated by, and with consent from those in power. The detective may get targeted in the same manner that you are, may cower but still demand payment. The last thing you need in the situation is to spend money for nothing.

Get a small camera. Cameras unnerve gang members. I have dealt with such devices and can state with certainty that they are their worst enemy. I remember when every day from the early morning till dusk a gang member would occasionally go as far as my backyard to check whether my window was open. This is because the neighbor who lived below would let loose wafts of poisonous substances through his window that would drift up and, depending upon the direction of the wind, into my room, that would otherwise be lost into the atmosphere if my window was closed. As soon as it was verified that I had my window open, and was in a compromised position so that I could not run fast enough to the source of the problem, the gasses would start wafting in, with immediate consequences. He stopped coming to the window when he realized I had been taking photographs of him.

Another time I noticed that an unusually large number of people would be standing at this bus station that I always used when going home in the evening. I realized that there never used to be that many people the first days I had used the location. I suspected stalker activity, especially since they would almost always anticipate the moment I turned the corner to walk up to the station, even though the bus for the stand on this side of the road came from the opposite direction; the direction they were supposed to be looking in if they were waiting and anxious to get their ride home. One day, I whipped out a camera as soon as their heads turned in my direction, some 100 or so meters away. Within moments, the platform was cleared of the unlikely crowd, leaving only a handful of people.

An individual standing on the other side of the road who noticed what had happened just broke out laughing.

Be warned when you take a walk or go for a jog that harassers attempt to prevent positive activity. They will do anything to dissuade you from refreshing your senses in any way as this only increases their work load. Avoid taking such activities at moments when the streets are empty of people. The lack of passers by gives them the opportunity to attack you in a manner that may have a negative psychological effect on you, as such preventing that you repeat the positive activity.

I suddenly started to come up against very aggressive characters when I took to jogging in the late evening or early morning when very few people were about. I can deal with such characters as I myself am not very smooth at base. One day, however, I came up against a big, shaggy, mad looking dog. The dog was evidently disturbed as soon as it set eyes on me, but fortunately allowed me to pass. I made nothing of this first encounter because, even though it is very rare to just come up against a stray dog in a modern European city, people still own dogs, and the possibility of a dog straying always exists.

When this same scene was repeated three times too many, with three different messy looking dogs, I changed my routine and started going out only when I knew the streets were full of people. I also started avoiding jogging in parks since a lot of people allow their dogs to run free there, and I have witnessed a few occurrences where a jogger was attacked by a dog.

As if to confirm my suspicions, I noticed a sudden rise of a subtle kind of aggression. I got a few harsh whispers of violence here and there, a few people waiting for me to pass through a particular point who would repeat the same threatening statements, or others meant to discourage the jogging, and twice even got the feigned drawing of a gun as I passed, accompanied by a few individuals coughing loudly on both sides of the road, confirming the aggression and indicating the person feigning was not alone. I knew what this was all about and didn't as much as blink at it. I knew that as long as I kept within the populated, busy areas, they could not come up with the mad dog routine, which is as close to imminent danger and a baited reaction as it gets.

Chapter 12
Conclusion

A lot has changed since the early days when I first became a victim of covert warfare. I remember times when those hounding and attacking me were so confident their activities would forever remain beyond the comprehension of most people, they would openly talk to me about articles I had written, e-mails I sent, what I was doing behind the privacy of my own walls, and even allude or react to what the attacks had done to my appearance, balance or behavior, while I was actually in the company of a lot of people.

They would sometimes make gestures, and even erupt into wild activities involving pedestrians or cars, in a busy neighborhood without the population connecting me to the activity. They could do this not only because they knew only I would know what was meant, since the content of the message was familiar to me alone, but because of the low level of awareness of this phenomenon that existed at the time in the populace at large.

This has changed significantly over time. Nowadays, accounts by victims of covert warfare are not rare, and the number of people in society wary of such harassing campaigns has increased to the point I have observed a noticeable decrease in the number of overt displays of such terrorism, save for those rare but repetitive instances when I come up against a couple of young men who wonder in frustration "why they just don't send in the bigger boys?"

I have observed that though more people have become aware of the ways of this particular world, there remains a degree of fear out there that stems from lack of knowledge on how to protect self from such attacks. As a result, people are not likely to dare stand up for their rights for fear of reprisal, meaning they would rather comply with what they know is unreasonable; with the result the entirety of the group sinks deeper into the chains of destructive oppression.

The few individuals who will inevitably dare to start movements, or even write positively and enlighteningly on the human condition, are ill prepared for the arsenal that will be unleashed against them, and will inevitably end up succumbing to cancers of all kinds, sudden strokes, mental degeneration, or will be taken out in arguments with wild strangers on the streets.

Every process has its stages, and the current level in the fight against covert warfare is that of enabling more awareness in the public at large of the practice. This is the reason there are currently an overabundance of first hand accounts on the subject, and a lot of books detailing the development of the methods and weapons used, rather than those giving methods on effective defense against such violence. Providing evidence of the existence of the phenomenon is seen as more important.
The fight for freedom from oppression and the need for release from torture and gradual death are however ongoing processes that I believe are intricately tied to the success of the process of increasing awareness. By providing people with knowledge on effective defense against covert warfare, more will be willing to stand up for what they believe in, while less people will have to endure the torture or die. Once the fight for freedom or the fight to escape from torture are advanced, general public awareness of covert warfare will also be advanced. It is after all the very people wanting to, or standing up for their rights, and the rights of others, and others fighting to free themselves from the torture covert warfare brings whom the public eventually relies on for the spread of this awareness.

I believe that once information on defense against covert warfare is made general; the more people come up with ever more genial and simple methods of ensuring that one is immune to attacks of this nature, the less the possibility will be of the practice continuing, at least not to the same level we have seen today. The success of the practice depends on the success level of attacks. Once people learn how to protect themselves, those who rely on this form of terrorism for control will have to figure out another method of keeping people down, otherwise the war will have been exposed.

I hope adding the little bit I have learnt along the way, by direct and indirect exposure to the beast, will enable a lot of people all over the world who are engaged in activities that could get them marked for such attacks, are already under covert attack, or contemplating activities that could attract such wrath, to be prepared for what is out there. I hope the knowledge I provide here presents the beginning many have sought to formidable movements against oppression of the many by a few.

Furthermore, the knowledge here is open to scrutiny, and can be corrected, improved or expanded upon, hopefully initiating a race that fosters the amount of knowledge on self defense against covert warfare. This will enable people to hold their own come what may, and be that more resolved and successful when they decide to stand up for their rights or such. Rouge groups will then find it that much harder to oppress the greater population through simple conspiracies relying on secrecy, involving chemical, biological and other attacks on either the entirety of the group or key individuals, as people will have the knowledge to identify such attacks, and the means to defend themselves against such evil.

Power must always be held by the grassroots of the people.

Bibliography

Bowart, W. (1978)"Operation Mind Control". New York: Dell Publishing Co.

Snow, R. (1998) "Stopping a Stalker". Plenum Press

Donner, F. J. (1990) "Protectors of Privilege". University of California Press

Donner, F. J. (1980) "The Age of Surveillance". Alfred A. Knopf Inc.

Dyer, J. (1998) "Harvest of Rage". Westview Press

Nickson, E. (1994) "The Monkey Puzzle Tree". Toronto: Alfred A. Knopf

Schnabel, J. (1997) "Remote Viewers: The Secret History of America's Psychic Spies". New York: Dell

Thomas, G. (1989) "Journey into Madness. The Secret Story of Secret CIA Mind Control and Medical Abuse". New York: Bantam

Scheflin, A.W., & Opton, E.M. (1978) "The Mind manipulators". New York: Paddington Press

Gillmor, D. (1987) I Swear By Apollo. Dr. Ewen Cameron and the CIA-Brainwashing Experiments. Montreal: Eden press

Collins, A. (1988/1998) "In the Sleep Room. The Story of CIA Brainwashing Experiments in Canada". Toronto: Key Porter Books

Marks, J. (1988) "The Search for the Manchurian Candidate". New York: W.W. Norton

Faden, R.R. (1995) Final Report. Advisory Committee on Human Radiation Experiments. Washington, DC: US Government Printing Office

Simpson, C. (1993) "The Splendid Blonde Beast. Money, Law, and Genocide in the Twentieth Century". New York: Grove Press

Simpson, C. (1988) "Blowback. The First Full Account of America's Recruitment of Nazis, and the Disastrous Effect on Our Domestic and Foreign Policy". New York: Weidenfeld and Nicolson

Hunt, L. (1991) "Secret Agenda. The United States Government, Nazi Scientists, and Project Paperclip". 1945 to 1990. New York: St. Martin's Press

Condon, R. (1959/1988)"The Manchurian Candidate". New York: Jove Books

Ross, Colin A. MD , "BLUEBIRD Deliberate Creation of Multiple Personality by Psychiatrists"

Morehouse, D. (2001) "Psychic Warrior". Saint Martin's Press

Glick, B. "War at Home". South End Press

Lawson, D. (2001) "Terrorist Stalking in America". Scrambling News

Rutz, C. (July 2001) "A Nation Betrayed". Fidelity Publishing,

Davenport, N. Ph.D., Schwartz R.D. and Elliott, G.P. (2002) "Mobbing, Emotional Abuse in the American Workplace". Civil Society Publishing

Marks, J.D. Norton, W.W. & Company (August 1991) "The Search for the Manchurian Candidate: The CIA and Mind Control". Reissue edition

Sweeney, H.M. (January 1999) "The Professional Paranoid". Feral House

Hirigoyen, Marie-France, Marx, H., Moore, T. (November 15, 2000) "Stalking the Soul: Emotional Abuse and the Erosion of Identity" Helen Marx Books

Erwin, S.I. (Digital - September 1, 2001) "Directed-Energy Weapons Promise 'Low Cost Per Kill' : An article from: National Defense"

Analysis by Fessler, E.A. (Hardcover - February 1, 1980) "Directed-Energy Weapons: A Juridical Analysis"

Wollmann, G. (Digital - April 30, 2003) "Directed energy weapons: Fact or fiction? : An article from: Military Technology"

Kalfoutzos, A. (Spiral-bound - 2002) "Free Electron and Solid State Lasers Development for Naval Directed Energy"

Iannini, R.E. "Electronic Gadgets for the Evil Genius : 28 Build-It-Yourself"

Gurstelle, W. (Hardcover - January 3, 2006) "Adventures from the Technology Underground : Catapults, Pulsejets, Rail Guns, Flamethrowers, Tesla Coils, Air Cannons, and the Garage Warriors Who Love Them"

Bischof, M. (1995) "Biophotons - The Light in Our Cells". German publisher: Zweitausendeins, Frankfurt

Bachechi, Orie (1982) "When Light Touches Many Changes Take Place". Kiva, Inc., 912 Broadway N.E., Albuquerque, NM 87102

Bachechi, Orie (1984) Personal Communication, Albuquerque, NM: Kiva, Inc.
Beall, Paula T. (1979) "Applications of Cell Biology to an Understanding of Biological Water" in Cell-Associated Water, (Drost-Hansen, W. and James S. Clegg; Eds.) New York: Academic Press

Clegg, James S. (1979) "Metabolism and the Intracellular Environment: The Vincinal-Water Network Model" in Cell-Associated Water, (Drost-Hansen, W. and James S. Clegg; Eds.) New York: Academic Press

Cook, Maurice B. (1980) "The Inert Gases". Toronto, Canada: Marcus Books

Davis, A.R. & W.C. Rawls (1979) "The Magnetic Blueprint of Life". Smithtown, NY: Exposition Press

Davis, A.R. & W.C. Rawls (1975) "The Magnetic Effect". Smithtown, NY: Exposition Press

Gauquelin, M. (1969) "The Cosmic Clocks". London: Peter Owen

Koch, William F. (1961) "The Survival Factor in Neoplastic and Viral Diseases". p. 16, pp. 278 & 288

Levine, S.A. and P.M. Kidd (1985) "Antioxidant Adaptation: Its Role in Free Radical Pathology". San Leandro, CA: Biocurrents Div., Allergy Research Group (400 Preda St., San Leandro, CA 94577)

Ling, G.N. (1969) "A New Model for the Living Cell: A Summary of the Theory and Recent Experimental Evidence in its Support" in International Review of Cytology 26, pp. 1-61

Maugh II, Thomas H. (1978) "Soviet Science: A Wonder Water From Kaza". Science 202, p. 414 (8/27/78)

Mikesell, Norman (1974) "Cellular Regeneration". pp. 2-16

Peschel, G. & P. Belouschek (1979) "The Problem of Water Structure in Biological Systems". Cell-Associated Water, (edited by W. Drost-Kansen & James S. Clegg) NY: Academic Press

Pierralos, J.C. (1971) "The Energy Field in Man and Nature". NY: Institute of Bioenergetic Analysis, p. 18

Ray, John (September 1984) Tapes from John Ray Lectures at Boulder, Colorado.

Rees, M.L. Lambdoid, "Cell Salt Line". p. 26 & 27

Richards, Shine E.E. (1983) "Earth Power Spectrum and Its Potential As A Usable Energy Source". Pie Town, NM

Richards, Shine E.E. (1984) "Multi-Octave Harmonic Interconnections". Pie Town, NM

Schul, Bill & Ed Pettit (1975) "The Secret Power of Pyramids". NY: Ballantine Books

Sykes, Egerton (1964) "The Keely Mystery". London: Markham House Press LTD.

Szent-Gyorgyi, A. (1973) "Electrons, Molecules, Biology and Cancer" in Acta Biochem et Biophysic Academy of Science, (Hungary) 8, pp. 117-127

Wiggins, P.M. (1972) "Intracellular pH and the Structure of Cell Water" Journal of Theoretical Biology 37, pp. 363-371

Glossary

Bureaucratic Capture: A growing phenomenon observed around the world where senior bureaucrats control elected ministers rather than the other way around, due in large part to their permanent occupancy.

Jew Baiting: The practice in the Germany of the 30's to systematically harass a Jew in order to elicit a reaction or response that would lead to their arrest, after which it was easy to send the arrestee on to a concentration camp. At the time in Germany, before the Final Solution, Jews enjoyed full citizen rights, and could as such not be arrested on racial grounds.

Cause Stalking: Term derived from the old practice in the Christian church of covertly harassing sinners in order to force them to repent, or force undesirables to leave the group.

COINTELPRO (Counter Intelligence Program): A program of the United States Federal Bureau of Investigation that was initially designed to "increase factionalism, cause disruption and win defections" inside the Communist Party U.S.A. (CPUSA). It was soon extended to include disruption of the Socialist Workers Party, African-American nationalist groups such as the Black Panther Party and the Nation of Islam, Martin Luther King Jr.'s Southern Christian Leadership Conference, and the entire New Left socio-political movement, which included antiwar, community, and religious groups. It's methods included infiltration, psychological warfare from the outside, harassment through the legal system, extralegal force and violence: The program was secret until 1971, when an FBI field office was burglarized by a group of left-wing radicals calling themselves the "Citizens' Commission to Investigate the FBI". Several dossiers of files were taken and the information passed to news agencies.

Conscientious Objector: A person whose beliefs are incompatible with a role in the armed forces because they are either pacifist or antimilitarist, who objects to a particular war for any reason whatsoever, or whether they are reacting to what they view as offensive or defensive aggression. The opposition to war need not be absolute and total, but may depend on circumstance. The only real criterion that defines a conscientious objector is that the individual is sincerely following the dictates of their conscience.

Directed Energy Weapon: Classified or unclassified electronic devises with potentially lethal consequences that utilize either electro magnetic fields or various radio frequencies, of which microwave frequencies, to do harm to the victim.

Extremely High Frequency (EHF): The highest radio frequency band. EHF runs the range of frequencies from 30 to 300 gigahertz, above which electromagnetic radiation is considered to be low (or far) infrared light, also referred to as Terahertz radiation. This band has a wavelength of one to ten millimetres, giving it the name millimeter band or millimetre wave. Radio signals in this band are extremely prone to atmospheric attenuation, making them of very little use over long distances. Even over relatively short distances, rain fade is a serious problem, caused when absorption by rain reduces signal strength.

Extremely Low Frequency (ELF): Radio frequencies from 3 to 30 Hz, operating in the same range as the brain's frequency of 14 Hz. They can as such be used to influence behavior. They are used by the US Navy and Soviet/Russian Navy to communicate with submerged submarines.

Faraday Cage: An enclosure designed to exclude electromagnetic fields. It is an application of Gauss' law, one of Maxwell's equations. Gauss's law describes the distribution of electrical charge on a conducting form, such as a sphere, a plane, a torus, etc. Intuitively, since like charges repel each other, charge will "migrate" to the surface of the conducting form. The application is named after physicist Michael Faraday, who built the first Faraday cage in 1836, to demonstrate his finding. Faraday was the experimentalist who described the physical concepts formulated in Maxwell's equations.

Gaslighting: Name derived from the 1944 movie "Gaslight". It is a method of psychological harassment similar to that used in the film by the character Charles Boyer against his wife when he tries to contrive incidents designed to make it appear as though she is delusional.

Hanging: The name given to the phenomenon of citizen harassment and elimination in England.

Manchurian Candidate: The name comes from the book "The Manchurian Candidate" written in 1959 by Richard Condon. It refers to an individual who has undergone brainwashing and/or mind control designed to create a "Sleeper" personality within that individual that can be activated by either remote control; exposure to specific events, milieus, images, or persons.

Mentacide: Term defined by the coiner psychologist Dr. Bobby Wright as the deliberate and systematic destruction of a group's minds with the ultimate objective being the extirpation of the group.

MKULTRA (also known as MK-ULTRA): The code name for a CIA mind- control research program that used unwilling, and sometimes unwitting subjects as guinea pigs, first brought to wide public attention by the U.S. Congress (Church Committee), and a presidential commission (Rockefeller Commission). It began in the 50s, and continued till the late 1960s. There is a lot of published evidence that the project involved not only the use of drugs to manipulate persons, but also the use of electronic signals to alter brain functioning.

Predatory Gangstalking: A criminal phenomenon referring to a group of loosely affiliated people who, in an organized and systematic manner, relentlessly invade an individual's life on a continuous basis, to an extreme degree, as part of their lifestyle. While each individual Gang-Stalker does his or her small part, what defines Predatory Gang-Stalking is the collective intent to do harm.

Stockholm Syndrome: The name comes from the Norrmalmstorg robbery of Kreditbanken at Norrmalmstorg, Stockholm in which the bank robbers held bank employees hostage from August 23 to August 28, 1973. It is a psychological response often seen in a hostage, similar to "battered woman syndrome", child abuse cases, and bride kidnapping, in which the victim bonds with the victimizer. In the case of the robbery, the hostage exhibits apparent loyalty to the hostage- taker, in spite of the danger and risks the hostage has been put in.

Whistle Blower: An employee, former employee or member of an organization who reports misconduct within the entity they are a part of in the above named ways to people or entities in society with the power to take corrective action.

Generally the misconduct is a violation of law, rule, regulation and/or a direct threat to public interest or safety. "External whistleblowers" are those who report misconduct within entities they either are a part of, for example as employees, or they are not a part of but have insight into crucial activities, to outside persons or entities such as lawyers, the media, law enforcement or watchdog agencies, whereas "internal whistleblowers" report misconduct of one employee to another employee or superior within the company, organization or agency.

© 2006 Mukazo Mukazo Vunda

Made in United States
Orlando, FL
30 October 2024